A LONG WINTER

A Long Winter

COLM TÓIBÍN

PICADOR

First published 2005 by Tuskar Rock Press

This edition published 2025 by Picador
an imprint of Pan Macmillan
The Smithson, 6 Briset Street, London ECIM 5NR
EU representative: Macmillan Publishers Ireland Ltd, 1st Floor,
The Liffey Trust Centre, 117–126 Sheriff Street Upper,
Dublin 1 DO1 YC43
Associated companies throughout the world

ISBN 978-1-0350-7984-1

1 3 5 7 9 8 6 4 2

A CIP catalogue record for this book is available from the British Library.

Typeset in Adobe Garamond Pro by Palimpsest Book Production Limited, Falkirk, Stirlingshire
Printed and bound in the UK using 100% Renewable Electricity
by CPI Group (UK) Ltd

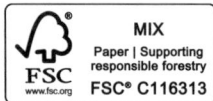

MIX
Paper | Supporting
responsible forestry
FSC
www.fsc.org
FSC® C116313

Visit **www.picador.com** to read more about
all our books and to buy them.

A LONG WINTER

1

Even as the days grew darker, the wind was mild. Miquel watched from the bedroom window as his father and Jordi walked along the lane which ran from the lower fields up to the barn. They were both in shirtsleeves as though it were a summer's day.

'We'll have no winter this year,' his father had said over dinner the previous evening, 'the priests have announced it as our reward for constant prayer and kindness to our neighbours.'

Miquel had managed a laugh to please his father, a role normally played by Jordi. But Jordi and their mother had remained silent. Jordi seldom spoke now and responded with hardly even a gesture if anyone said a word to him.

On Saturday he would be taken to La Seu for a special haircut and be gone by Tuesday to do his military service. He would be away for two years.

A week earlier, when the final summons arrived, Jordi had asked Miquel what it was like, travelling by lorry to Lérida, being handed a uniform, spending the night in a barracks like a prisoner, eating their food, and travelling by train to Zaragoza or Madrid or Valladolid, wherever they decided to billet you.

'You've just described it,' Miquel said.

'Yes, but what's it like?' Jordi asked.

Miquel shrugged and held Jordi's gaze; there was nothing to be said about it. It was not worth remembering or commenting on. Without realizing, he had let his mind wander over certain details from his own two years in uniform, but he stopped himself suddenly when he saw that Jordi had become frightened.

Jordi, who seemed to spend most of his last days at home petting his dog Clua or playing with him, had not spoken to Miquel since then but he did not seem angry with him or in a sulk with him; rather, he understood that

2

since they could not speak easily about the ordeal ahead of him, then they had better not speak at all. Even in the bedroom they shared, as they undressed or prepared to turn off the light, neither of them said a word. Miquel was deeply aware that the other single bed in the small room would soon be empty. He supposed that his mother would strip the sheets from it and leave the mattress bare during his brother's absence.

More than with fear or hunger or constant discomfort, he associated his years of military service with dreams of home. In the early months, as he received useless training under the punishing sun, he wondered why he had never viewed his life with his family in the village as precious and fragile. He dreamed of cold dawns, being woken by his father to get up and come with him in the jeep to the uplands where the flocks of sheep were summering. He dreamed about Jordi, who loved his sleep, deciding whether or not he would come with them. He dreamed about his own bed, the familiar room, the sounds of night and morning, the scops owl near the window in summer, the creaking of the floorboards as his mother moved in the night, the bringing of the flocks down to the barns in the winter, the narrow street of the village full of their cries.

Every day he had planned his return, longed for it in detail, lived in the ordinary future where the smallest domestic detail – the sound of a jeep starting up, a chainsaw, a hunter's gun or a dog's bark – would signify that he had returned, that he had survived. He had imagined this homecoming in all its satisfying comfort and freedom so closely that he had put no thought into how soon Jordi's turn would come, how soon his brother would have to submit himself to the humiliation of the haircut and the standing in the cold waiting for the lorry to take him to Lérida. Miquel knew how bad it would be for his brother, and it was as though some more vulnerable and innocent part of him were going to have the haircut, leaving an empty bed behind.

For the past week their mother had not been able to stay still. At times, it seemed to Miquel as if she were searching for something, moving around the kitchen and the long dining room and the storeroom. The great sporadic restlessness of hers had begun, he knew, as soon as he came back from the mili; he noticed it not long after his return. He did not think it had happened while he was away as Jordi had not mentioned it to him, and seemed too pre-occupied to notice it now.

Her inability to settle came and went as though governed by the weather. In these last days, as Jordi prepared to go, the jittery, nervous movements had intensified, she seemed to Miquel like a strange, hungry animal who was living with them, barely able to cook or set the table, barely able to feed her hens and rabbits and geese. He wondered why she was so upset about Jordi's going; she had not behaved like this in the time before he left.

Now, however, as they had breakfast before the journey down to La Seu, she sat still at the table, wearing her good clothes, nervous and not speaking, but more composed than she had been for some weeks.

He had been so charged with happiness at coming home, he thought, that he had not bargained for this, the sitting into the back seat of the jeep with Jordi beside him and his mother and father in front as though they were transporting Jordi to be sold and slaughtered. But once the jeep got going, moving through familiar territory, there were moments when he fooled himself in thinking that this was an ordinary visit to La Seu on a market day with baskets of eggs to sell and a list of things to buy, then the dull fact of Jordi's departure would hit him again and the old dread would return.

His father was to accompany Jordi to the barber's, its owner a man known for his solemnity, and understood to be a communist, having served years in prison after the war. Thus he could be guaranteed to make no jokes or gleeful, mocking comments as he cut Jordi's hair according to army regulation. He would maintain his mournful tone and preserve, as much as he could, Jordi's dignity.

That day they had no eggs or poultry to sell, but groceries to buy. They would even have to purchase vegetables since their own garden had yielded hardly anything in the past weeks. Miquel and his mother, carrying two shopping baskets each, did not stop at the barber's, arranging instead to meet Jordi and his father in the body of the market in an hour's time.

Once they were alone with each other, his mother's step

was lighter, she seemed almost happy as she faced into the market, greeting a number of stall-holders warmly, familiarly, announcing proudly to one of them that she had nothing to sell today, she was here only to buy, and laughing when the woman retorted that if more people did the same then all the stall-holders would become rich.

Then she left him, telling him to wait for her, there was something she needed to buy. It would not take long, she said. Her parting was abrupt, as though she felt that he would argue with her if she stayed a moment longer. He watched her slipping between two stalls, still carrying the baskets.

He wished she had given him something to do. He could easily have gone and bought the oil, or ordered the bottled gas so that it would be ready when they drove by at the end of the day. He watched the flower-sellers, alone among the stall-holders in not having a queue to buy their wares, the two women contented-looking. He wondered who would have the spare money to buy flowers.

Slowly, as he waited, he grew tired and bored. He supposed that his mother had gone to the butcher's or the poultry shop where there could be long queues, or even to buy something quite private at the pharmacy. After a while, he made his way, as his mother had done, between two of the stalls to the line of shops on the other side of them where he thought he could find her, believing that he could wait with her. If he saw that she was in the pharmacy, he would stay outside. The thought of standing beside her in a line of people, carrying the bags for her, pleased him. She had a way with people – strangers, or shopkeepers – a sort of charm which drew people towards her, and made him enjoy being with her in those moments when she smiled at someone or made a passing remark; it almost made him proud.

She was not in the queue at the butcher's, which was long. He had decided to walk up the street towards the poultry shop when he suddenly saw her with her back to the plate-glass window of a bar he had never noticed before. He was about to knock on the window, expecting her to turn and smile at him, but the expression on the face of the bar owner made him stop for a moment. Miquel watched as the owner counted out some coins and moved to a row of bottles at the back of the bar. He filled a large glass, the sort normally used for water, with a thin yellow liquid, like pale tea or light sherry, and brought it back to Miquel's mother. It was, he guessed, a fino, or a cheap wine, or a muscatel. He saw her grip the glass and finish it in two gulps; and, before he turned away, he noticed two empty glasses beside her on the counter, the same type of tumbler that she had just drunk from. He quickly went back to the spot where she had left him earlier, where she soon found him, her face flushed, her eyes bright, and they began the day's shopping.

He knew what he had seen; he understood now why she had gone alone, leaving him waiting; it was clear to him why she was so happy, almost carefree, as she made her first purchases. He also realized that he had known this vaguely for some time – the smells from her breath, the mood swings, the restlessness, were evidence enough to suggest something – but he had not allowed himself to put a name to it. She had downed the tumbler of wine the way a thirsty person would drain a glass of water. She must have done the same to the other two. There was no other explanation. He wondered if this would be enough for her, how long she could keep going on these tumblers of wine or sherry or whatever it was, if she would need more soon, or something stronger. He wondered if his father knew about this, or if Jordi knew. He supposed that their father must know, since he shared a bed with her every night, knew all her moods and movements. He was not sure, however, of the extent of his mother's drinking; maybe it merely happened in the early part of market day in La Seu, but he did not think so. And even if it were bad and went back a long time, it would be typical of his father not to mention it, or make anything of it, to store it up instead as another amusing aspect of the world.

When they had bought all the vegetables and were walking out of the bread shop, his mother spoke to him, moving her head carefully away, he noticed, so that he would not smell her breath.

'When you went to the mili,' she said, 'I thought you would never come back, but the time was actually short. It won't seem long at all before Jordi is back too.'

They stood in the queue at the butcher's, where he had

imagined finding her before. It was all different now, even though only fifteen minutes had passed. He listened to her voice and watched her move with a new suspicion. Maybe, he thought, he had drawn conclusions too quickly. Maybe these were her only few glasses of the week, and she was, he thought, entitled to look forward to them, living in a village where there was no bar, no shop, nothing except hostile neighbours and a long winter.

His mother knew the butcher's wife, having often sold her rabbits. When she informed her now about Jordi going to the mili, the owner's wife and the women all around commiserated with her and, on noticing Miquel, smiled and said that she was lucky to have this one, so tall and handsome. She would be lucky if he were not married soon, the owner's wife said. One of the women joined the conversation to say that she had a daughter of the same age and they would make a great match. Miquel smiled and said he had no time for things like that, he would have too much work to do now that Jordi was going.

Jordi was wearing a cap when they met him. He grinned at Miquel and put his arm around him. They walked with their parents past the stalls which sold cheese and olives towards a small bar near the bus station where they ordered bocadillos and soft drinks.

'You'll have to take off your cap eventually,' Miquel said.

'I'm going to wait until the very last minute,' Jordi replied.

They ate quietly, the silence interrupted only by their father's views, spoken almost to himself, on the clientele, or the delays in the service, or the price of things, including communist haircuts. Miquel saw no reason to respond, and was surprised to see Jordi following suit. When he was away, he thought, his father's comments on all matters was one thing he did not miss, but Jordi was softer, more willing to create harmony, and he would, Miquel knew, miss everything as soon as he left them. He watched his mother gazing happily around her, sipping a glass of water.

Later, they separated, their mother going alone to purchase household goods and the men going to get bottled gas and to look at a saw their father had noticed in a shop window. Miquel was sure that his father did not need a new saw, but, perhaps more than any of them now, he needed something with which to distract himself. Miquel studied him as, suggesting affluence and serious intent, he sought and received the shop assistant's full attention, and then had the saw removed from the window. He watched his father demand a block of wood so that the saw could be tested; his father stood impatiently, with the air of a master woodcutter, until it was brought. When it came, he knelt and applied the saw, frowning regularly at the assistant and his two sons, ignoring the small audience which had built up around him as he set out to prove, Miquel realized, that the saw's blade was as good as blunt. Having done so to his own satisfaction, he stood up and wiped the sawdust from his hands.

When they drove to collect their mother, Miquel and Jordi descended to fetch her packages. She told them that the oil was not ready. It would, she said, have to be delivered during the week. When their father suggested that they go to another shop, she said no, they had already paid for it. It was, she said, the best oil and the best price, and the shopkeeper had promised faithfully that it would be delivered in a few days. Miquel noticed that she came close to losing her self-possession as she spoke, explaining what would happen with the oil in too much detail. Their father, already driving out of the town, said that a grocery shop without oil was like a winter without snow, it was not natural. Not natural at all, he laughed to himself.

Jordi would have two more days with them. That night, when they went to their bedroom and in casual silence prepared for bed, Miquel took in everything so that he might remember it in all its detail – the closing of the door so that they were in the room alone together, the creaking of the floorboards, the parcelling out of the small space so that they did not get in one another's way as they undressed, their soft shadows on the wall. Jordi was slower in his movements than he was, Miquel noted as though for the first time, but tidier also, he loved folding things. He kept his pyjamas folded neatly under his pillow. In the mili, in the long dormitories in a vast barracks somewhere, such habits could be easily mocked.

He watched Jordi who had his back to him quietly taking off his pullover and leaving it on top of the chest of drawers for the morning. Miquel was usually in bed before his brother. He was careful not to look directly at Jordi as he changed into his pyjamas; instead, he put his hands behind his head and studied the ceiling, making comments on things, much as his father did, sometimes doing imitations of his father's harmless daily grumblings, to Jordi's shocked delight.

This familiar life was now ending. Jordi would come back eventually, but he would have to leave soon afterwards to find work, begin his own life. The house and the land would be left to Miquel, as his father, in turn, had been left the house and farm by his father. Nights like this would not come again. There must be people, he realized, who relished this change, who longed for the first night of a marriage, all the newness and separation, the moving to a new house, the making of large decisions. His mother must have lain at night in her village over the mountain, knowing it would be her last night there. His father must have seen his own brothers go, one by one. Miquel understood that he himself had no interest in change; he wanted things to remain as they were. By the time he had thought this through and begun to puzzle over its implications,

Jordi had fallen asleep. Miquel could imagine his innocent white face and his black hair, cut down to the scalp; he could hear his peaceful breathing. He almost wanted to touch him, move towards him and put his hand tenderly for one moment on his face.

Their mother was busy in the kitchen all the following day as she prepared a supper for the four of them, making a terrine with marinated rabbit and carrots and onions that Jordi loved, and roasting a stuffed goose for the main course. As Miquel came in and out of the kitchen, passing her as she worked, he looked for signs of a bottle near the work table or a glass of wine or brandy close to her, but he could see nothing.

That evening, she put a white tablecloth on the good old table, and set it as though her brother and sister-in-law were making a visit from Pallosa over the mountain, or one of her husband's brothers had come from Lérida. In the late afternoon, Miquel had noticed a bottle of white wine already opened; he supposed she needed it for the cooking, but now when he looked again he saw that it was gone.

Their mother brushed her hair and put on fresh clothes;

their father wore his suit and a white shirt. It would have been easier, Miquel thought, if one or two of the neighbours had called, or were invited to eat with them, but too much had happened in the village over the years for that. While all the neighbours would know the date of Jordi's departure, it would not be mentioned, it would remain part of the heavy silence which had gathered since the row about the water. They would eat alone.

On nights like this he saw his parents young, his father attentive, full of sweetness in the way he lit the candles and passed food and poured wine; his mother would be free now to talk about her own mother and the food she made for different occasions and what was said about her, and the parties in the old village, the good neighbours they had there. She would do this carefully, not implying any criticism of the life she lived here, which they were celebrating more than any past life.

2

One morning after Jordi had left, Miquel surprised his mother by coming silently into the kitchen as she was gulping from a glass. She put it down hurriedly. He tried to get close to her to see what he could smell from her breath, but she seemed to keep away from him deliberately, moving quickly out to the rabbit house and the hen house. As soon as she left, however, he found the glass. It was empty, but the residual smell was of strong wine; to his nostrils that morning the smell was pungent, almost rotten. He left the glass back where he had found it in case she came suddenly back into the room.

His mother had left Jordi's bed untouched for the first few days. Only the folded pyjamas under the pillow were missing. It was when she took the sheets and blankets from the bed, leaving a bare pillow and a bare mattress, that Miquel dreaded going up to his bedroom at night. A few times in the first days he managed to forget that Jordi was gone; he thought he heard him breathing in the night, and on one of the mornings, when the first sounds could be heard, he found himself looking over at his brother's bed to see if Jordi was awake yet.

Since the days remained dry and the sun was warm, his father expressed the view that they should keep busy, repair a wall of the barn, work they might never do, he said, but always plan to do until their barns were rubble and the sheep were shivering with the cold out in the fields all night. He mentioned Castellet, one of his neighbours, whose laziness was a constant source of interest. If we don't repair the barns, we'll end like Castellet. Saying the name alone appeared to give his father pleasure, made him smile in the calm, amused way to which Miquel had become so accustomed.

The work was tough, with heavy stones to remove and replace and beams to shore up and slates to take down. His father, who had worked as a stone cutter, repointed the stones and cut new ones which he had bought from the owner of a ruined barn in a nearby village and painstakingly transported to his own holding. He gradually made clear that he planned to dismantle one whole side of the barn, using cheap bricks on the inside and facing it with stone. Miquel was doing all the lifting and carrying, his father having found a place in the sun where he could chisel and shape and flatten. Each time Miquel passed him with a loaded wheelbarrow, or presented him with a new pile of stones, he had remarks to make, on the habits of the neighbours, or the poorness of the brick, or the durability of the stone, or the shortness of the lambing season, or the lunch which might be waiting for them, or where Jordi might be now and when they might hear from him.

When it went beyond two in the afternoon, and the sun disappeared behind the hills, it would grow bitterly cold, letting them know that, despite the bright days, they were in the depths of winter. Miquel tried to convince his father that they should not work after lunch, except the usual work with the animals and their feed, but his father insisted that another hour each day would make all the difference. Once they started, however, they seldom stayed long, his father nodding and smiling when Miquel stood in front of him announcing that he had carried his last stone of the day.

On one of those days when Miquel returned to the house in the afternoon earlier than expected he found his mother sitting at the kitchen table. She did not look up when he came in. Normally, she sat down in the morning to have a cup of chocolate but otherwise, he knew, she disliked sitting down until after supper. She preferred moving around all day, cooking, washing clothes and looking after her hens, rabbits and geese. He pretended at first not to notice her, filling a glass of water from the tap, but when he turned he saw that she was sitting with her arms wrapped around herself and was rocking back and forth. When he asked her if she was all right, she did not look at him.

'Get your father,' she said.

When Miquel came back with his father, she was still rocking, as though this were her only way of keeping the pain, whatever it was, from overwhelming her. She did not look up.

'What is it?' his father asked.

'You know what it is,' she said calmly, and recoiled when his father made to touch her.

'Was it both of you, or just you?' she asked.

'Just me,' his father said.

'What did you do?' Miquel asked.

'Dumped the containers of wine just delivered, emptied them,' she said.

'I didn't see any wine,' Miquel said.

'You could barely call it wine,' his father said. 'Acid. You didn't see it because she hid it. I watched the whole adventure from the top floor of the low barn with those binoculars you brought back from the mili. They were delivering the oil, but it was just an excuse.'

'Spying on me,' his mother said.

'And what did you do?' Miquel asked his father.

'I went down,' his father said, 'when they had gone and I emptied it, all of it. And I put the containers back where they were, but they were empty now of their poison.'

'You know all about poison,' she said.

Miquel was surprised by the suddenness of her anger, her sharpness.

'I'm the one has to sleep with you,' his father said. 'And the smell of that stuff rotting you as you sleep.'

His mother continued to rock back and forth, as though they were not there. They stood close to her, Miquel noticing a look on his father's face, both sorry and nervous – concerned, it seemed to Miquel, that he had said too much and ready now to be softer with her.

'I am sorry,' his mother said quietly, 'that I ever knew any of you.' Her tone was definite, decisive.

Miquel's father looked at her puzzled.

'Any of us?'

'That's what I said. Did you not hear me?'

'Who do you mean?'

'I mean the people in this house.'

'Who? Let us know who you mean.'

'I mean everyone, but especially you.' She spoke quietly again. 'That's who I mean.'

'Well, there's no point in speaking to you, then, is there?' he asked.

'Are you going to replace what you threw out?' she asked.

'I am not.'

'Well, that's the end, then,' she said and began to cry.

As his father left the house, Miquel was unsure if he should remain. He watched his father from the window walking down towards the barn they were repairing. Miquel listened as his mother's crying grew louder, more uncontrolled. He moved closer to her and put his hand on her shoulder. Slowly, she moved her hand towards his, caught one of his fingers and caressed it and then took his whole hand in hers and held it. Her crying now stopped but she was still rocking gently back and forth.

3

His mother did not move and would eat nothing. When Miquel had lit the fire, and put extra kindling on it until it was blazing, he suggested that she sit near it. She allowed him to lead her there and put her sitting as though she were blind or had no will of her own. She insisted that she was not hungry. Asking her if she wanted something to drink would sound like a bitter joke at her expense so he did not ask her.

Miquel and his father sat at the table and had the soup left over from the previous day, and then ate some ham and tomatoes and bread. It was not the dinner they normally had, but they did not mention it or complain. When he was about to go to bed and he met his father on the upstairs landing, Miquel spoke quietly to him, proposing that they should go to La Seu in the morning and buy her some wine, better wine than the stuff the grocer had delivered, and tell her now that she could come with them if she wanted. His father put his arm around him before he replied.

'No, it's better like this. We did that when you were away. She has to stop altogether. That's what the doctor told us a few months ago, the only way to stop was to stop. Now, since she has no drink, she will stop. It's the best thing. She'll be fine in a few days.'

'How long has she been drinking?' Miquel asked.

'A few years.'

'How is it we never noticed?'

'We all noticed,' his father said.

'Jordi didn't,' Miquel replied.

'He did, son, he did,' his father said.

When he went back downstairs, his father followed him; they found his mother still sitting in front of the fire. She was shaking as though with the cold. Miquel left them and went to bed.

As he lay in bed with the light out, while hearing vague stirrings from the floor below him, he remembered how different Jordi was with him at first when they were alone in the bedroom after he came back from the mili. Before this Jordi and he had been natural and relaxed about undressing in front of each other, but Jordi would now cover himself if Miquel came in, or would sit awkwardly on the side of the bed taking off his shorts and putting on his pyjama-bottoms as modestly as if there were a woman in the room. Jordi and his father took time to get used to his homecoming, disguising the fact that they had managed without him, Jordi loath to hand over some of the jobs which naturally belonged to his older brother. Thus they did not tell him that his mother, while he was away, had become a hopeless drinker. In keeping the secret, they had treated him like a stranger.

In the night he heard their voices in the room below; his father's was calm but his mother's was high and whimpering. Eventually, they came to bed and there was silence for some time until he heard the floorboards creaking and one of them going downstairs again. Soon the other followed and the voices started again. He knew that he would not sleep. It was hard anyway since Jordi was absent from the other bed; it was the no sound coming from there kept him awake, the no snoring or rhythm of breathing, the no turning over which seemed to disturb him more than the wind, which appeared now to have changed direction, blowing fiercely from the north in the few hours before the dawn, rattling the window.

In the morning he found his father in the kitchen. His mother, he presumed, was in bed. His father began to shave, using the small mirror over the kitchen sink, working with slow concentration.

'Should we not go to La Seu and get her what she wants?' Miquel asked.

His father did not reply.

'Replace what was thrown out.' He raised his voice.

'No,' his father said, catching Miquel's eye in the mirror. 'She has to stop some day. The best day for everything is always today. Anyway, she's asleep now.'

He continued shaving even more slowly and carefully, as though this were a more pressing concern of his than any matter his son might care to raise. Miquel found some bread and rubbed some oil and tomato and salt into it, finding also a lump of cheese and cutting off a slice. He ate quickly, hungrily, before going outside to collect the eggs from the hen house, passing his father who did not speak to him.

Once in the shade, he noticed how intensely cold it had become; the water in the fenced-off piece of ground in front of the hen house was completely frozen. The sky was blue, but it was not the still, calm blue of earlier days, it was more that the clouds had been blown back by the wind, making the blue of the sky seemed exposed and raw. When he looked down towards the barns he saw that his father had found a sheltered spot in the sunlight. Miquel joined him and they spent the morning slowly facing the new brick of the barn with stone.

Before lunch they went to inspect the sheep, bringing down feed from the upper floor of the barn. They were not sure of the time, but, once they were finished with the sheep, Miquel was surprised that his mother had not called them in to eat. Then he remembered what had happened and wondered if she were still in bed or too distressed to cook for them.

When they came into the house, he knew that she had not been in the kitchen. Nothing had been touched or cleared away. Clua, he saw, had not been fed. His father went upstairs and then came down and said that she was not in their bedroom. By the time they had finished their first search of the house and the grounds around the barns and outhouses, Miquel knew that she had gone. Their leaving her all morning, not once going into the house, even to get a glass of water, or check her state of mind, seemed now like an invitation for her to go. As they searched once more, and this search too became futile, Miquel began to consider where she might have gone and how she might have travelled. She could not have taken refuge with any of their neighbours; nobody in the village would have known what to do were she to arrive on their doorstep, she had not been inside any of their houses for some years. There was no transport available out of the village, no bus until the main road ten or eleven kilometres away, and that service was irregular. Nobody would stop and collect her were she to walk towards La Seu, unless a stranger were to be in the area, which was unlikely.

She had, in any case, left them. When his father suggested searching the inside of the barns, Miquel shook his head. His mother would have had to walk right past them to get to the barns except for the short time they went to inspect the sheep, and even then they would have seen her. Her coat was gone and her good scarf and her boots. His father, even when Miquel had twice shown him the space where the missing coat had hung and the space where the missing boots had lain, went upstairs again and again in search of her, to the top loft, to the store, to the barn directly below them. Miquel sat down at the table, letting his father search for as long as he pleased, knowing that eventually he would have to sit down too and talk about what should be done now.

There were still ten or twelve houses inhabited in the village; nothing happened that was not noticed, the old people sat by windows watching, the few young men were in the fields or by the barns, the women did their house-work checking regularly on the weather. There were no children in any of the houses; most of the young had fled to the cities or bigger towns. Miquel and Jordi were the two youngest left in the place. They had been brought up to depend on no one around them, but it was only in recent years that the hostility between their father and the rest of the village had grown so intense that there was almost no contact with the neighbours. Their father had denounced three families for diverting water in the summer months. He had gone to Tremp and given evidence against them, while the other families, despite having water stolen from them, had spoken in their defence. The judge imposed fines. The feelings about the willingness of Miquel's father to betray them were sharp and fresh in the households that had to pay the fines. Their father took pleasure, if he could make one of his sons listen, in calling his neighbours liars and thieves. The neighbours, in turn, passed him every day without speaking.

Now, he and Miquel would have to go from house to house, their search for his mother an admission that all was not well in their home. They could not be sure, Miquel realized, that the neighbours would even tell them what they had seen. But it was the only thing they could do. So once his father had ceased his searching, they put their coats on and set out, being careful to begin with the closest neighbour so that no one would think they had any special friends or favoured household in the village.

Mateu at the Casa Raúl came to the door slowly, his fat belly in front of him. He was one of the men who had to pay the fine. He screwed his eyes up in distaste as soon as Miquel's father opened his mouth, giving no sign that he understood a word spoken. Instead, he studied their faces, taking his time to consider what he saw. Miquel believed at first that whether Mateu had seen his mother or not he would be no use to them. The problem would be how quickly they could move away from his door. Miquel nudged his father and nodded his head in the direction of the next house, but his father stood there, resting himself against the doorframe, waiting for something, neither repeating the question nor saying anything else as Mateu cleared his throat. Mateu's house was the closest to theirs; Mateu, Miquel imagined, had probably not left the house all day, he had good views from his windows and would have seen her easily no matter in what direction she had gone.

As they stood in the doorway, the sky darkened suddenly, blue-black clouds appeared over them, gathering in a low dense mass. The light became a dark purple and there was no wind. Miquel shivered. He knew that it meant snow; it would be the first of the year, late in coming, and all the more severe on a day as cold as this.

'I saw her going all right,' Mateu said, 'but there was no sign of her coming back.'

'Which direction?' Miquel's father asked.

'She took the road towards Coll del So.'

'But that leads nowhere,' his father said.

Mateu nodded.

It struck Miquel immediately that it led towards Pallosa, where his mother's brother still lived in the old family house; it could be reached in four or five hours.

'How long ago did you see her?' his father asked.

'She's gone a few hours,' Mateu said.

'What? Three or four?'

'Yes, three or four, or somewhere in between.'

The snow came down gently as the air darkened even further. The flakes were thick, they did not melt immediately on the back of Miquel's hand which he held out to test them. The jeep, he knew, could make its way along the narrow road which led to the small church at Santa Magdalena, and perhaps even further along the military road to Coll del So, but after that, he thought, his mother would make her way down to Pallosa along old tracks and pathways which no jeep could follow and no outsider could find. In three or four hours walking she could be still on the military road, but it was unlikely. More probably, she would have reached Coll del So and then she might even have started along the steeper tracks, and he knew that they must race to the jeep and drive as fast as they could along the winding road to these uplands where they kept their sheep in the summer, territory which remained unvisited in the winter.

'You won't get far now,' Mateu said to them as they moved away from his door.

'Are you certain she went that way?' Miquel called back to him.

'Ask the others, we all saw her.'

They walked back quickly to the house. As his father turned the jeep, Miquel ran into the house to fetch his binoculars.

'What are you doing with those?' his father asked.

Miquel looked down at them resting in his lap.

'I don't know . . . I thought . . .'

'We don't have time for thinking,' his father said.

They drove along the narrow road out of the village; the windscreen wipers were on full, but still the snow impaired their vision and the jeep's headlights caught sheets of whiteness. Had she been on the road coming towards them, even with her arms outstretched, they would not have seen her. It must have been clear to his father, Miquel knew, that there was little purpose in their journey. The only hope, Miquel thought, was that she had left later than Mateu had said. He considered that for a moment and then the possibility that she had walked slowly, or had turned back at some point, and then he let his mind linger over another possibility – that she had walked quickly and left even earlier than Mateu had said and was within reach of Pallosa, that she was clambering down the old paths as best she could. Moving slowly and carefully, watching each step. It was territory she knew; she was, Miquel thought, unlikely to make mistakes. But he was not sure. Perhaps the paths down the slopes would be all hidden now and every step treacherous.

His father worked hard to manage the jeep as it began to sway and slide. Even when the snow was not blown hard against the windscreen, they could see it falling in dense waves and building up on the road in front of them so that after a while they were driving on a thick blanket of snow, which was gathering in strength as they moved forward. Soon it was obvious that their way would eventually be impeded, their way back made impossible.

Miquel knew that it would make sense for him to suggest they stop and turn, that their moving ahead was perhaps pointless and maybe even dangerous, but he knew also that if they turned and went home they would be facing into sheer emptiness, with no idea where his mother was and the long night ahead of them.

When there was a small clearing, his father, without

saying anything, tried to turn the jeep, believing, it seemed to Miquel, that the snow covered a level surface. But it merely covered a sharp dip between the road and the verge into which one of the front wheels now sank. His father cursed as Miquel got out of the jeep to see if he could ease the vehicle back onto the road. He watched the wheel revolve frantically, like a spider caught in water. In the end, they had to find stones wherever they could and a short plank from the back of the jeep and settle these under the wheel; they were blinded by the snow as they scampered about the jeep. When he turned to avoid the driving snow, he found that it was blowing and swirling in all directions as though the four winds were competing with each other. They began to push the jeep once the wheel had been stabilized, trying to lift it back onto the road, but the wheels were stuck in the snow and would not easily move. They were, Miquel guessed, half an hour's walk from the village, maybe more in the snow, and he imagined, as his father revved the engine in one more large effort to move the jeep, that his mother, having avoided the worst of the weather, was now knocking gently on the door of her brother's house, the house where she was born. They loved her in that house and they would welcome her and in the morning they would find a way of sending a message to say that she was safe.

He heaved one more time as his father put sudden pressure on the accelerator. The jeep slid sideways; its four wheels were now on the road, still facing away from the village. His father shouted to him to get back in, he was going to try to turn the jeep again. He put it in neutral and let it inch forward as far as it could safely go and then he pulled up the handbrake and put it into reverse. He let the handbrake down and slowly accelerated. At first it did not move, and then the back wheels began to revolve in the snow until his father gave the accelerator fierce pressure and they moved back at speed, sliding on the road. But they were almost facing the village now; they could go back, cutting with difficulty through the settling snow on the ground and the gusts of thick snowflakes gathering on the windscreen as fast as the wipers could remove them.

Once home, they went through all the possibilities, how quickly she could walk, at what time she had left, how long it took along the road until you had to find the old paths which led down to Pallosa. Even in summer there were tough stretches, parts you had to scramble down rather than walk. She could, Miquel said, have turned back when the snow came. She knew how dangerous a snowstorm like this could be. Even if she were closer to Pallosa when it started, she might have thought that it was safer on the level track than on the slopes moving downwards, and even though it would take her hours, trudging through the snow, it might have been the wisest thing to do.

'If we went to La Seu,' Miquel said, 'we could ask the police there to find out if she arrived in Pallosa. We could report her as missing.'

His father sighed.

'I know she's alive somewhere,' he said.

Miquel did not answer him.

When a knock came to the door, he believed in the first instant that their troubles were over, she had come back. Then, however, he realized that she would not knock the door of her own house. Whoever had knocked remained outside. Perhaps they had found her or knew where she was. When his father went into the hallway and opened the door, Miquel saw that it was Josep Bernat and his wife. They had not come to this house, he knew, since the court case.

'We saw her going,' Josep said. 'We thought it was a strange time to be setting off. She had a bag with her.'

'A shopping bag,' his wife added.

'We noticed it because it was the wrong direction for shops.'

'She was going back to Pallosa, I suppose,' Miquel's father said.

'Could you not have driven her there?' Josep asked.

As his father sighed again, Miquel moved towards the window where he could see dense whirling snow still falling outside. The visitors remained standing; they had not been asked to take their coats off, nor offered any refreshment. Miquel could sense that Josep now regretted his last question. He smiled hesitantly at their neighbour as his father turned away.

'We could report her missing to the police in La Seu,' Miquel said.

'The road is probably impassable now and the phone lines from there might be down,' Josep replied. 'It'll be worse later because it's starting to freeze as well. They'll open the road in the morning, I hope.'

'Do you remember what time she left at?' Miquel asked.

'She didn't leave in time to get to Pallosa before the snow,' Josep replied.

'She could have turned back when it started,' Miquel said.

'It would be hard in that blizzard to have any sense of direction,' Josep said.

'Don't say anything more!' Miquel's father said.

'We were going to say that the men will all search for her when the light comes,' Josep's wife said. 'The minute there's light. But they can't search for her now. The snow has not done its worst yet. They cannot go out in the blizzard.'

'She's gone, then,' Miquel's father said, sitting down and sighing. 'No one could last the night in the open. She'll die of the cold.'

'You never can tell,' Josep said.

'We'll talk in the morning, then,' Miquel's father said.

'We can ask the police to check if she ever arrived in Pallosa.'

When Josep Bernat and his wife left the house, Miquel stood with his father watching them as they trudged through the snow. Then Miquel went outside to make sure that there was enough feed in the hen house, collecting eggs at the same time, and then feeding the rabbits and closing their shed for the night. At the doorway, he gave Clua, who seemed ravenous, some scraps. As his father sat silently at the table, he fried six eggs in oil, letting the oil splutter onto the tiles around the cooker, as his mother would never do. He cut some stale bread and brought some salt and oil and the one half-tomato that was left to the table. He put three fried eggs on a plate for his father and three for himself. As they ate in silence, Miquel thought over and over of the possibility that this was not really happening, it was a long dream he would soon wake from, or a scene which would change without warning as another knock came to the door or a jeep pulled up outside, or her face, smiling and nervous, appeared at the window as they both stood up to greet her, their food half eaten.

In the morning he woke to the sound of boots on the stairs, boots on the floorboards below and men's voices. He quickly dressed in the freezing bedroom before opening the shutters to a world of pure glaring whiteness. He went downstairs. Five or six men from the village were there, one of them had brought a pot of coffee and some brandy. His father, he noticed, looked shrunken and cowed beside these other men. He realized that in all his life he had seldom seen other men in this kitchen, his uncle a few times and the postman, or men coming to sell or repair something, but they were always somehow in the shadows. These men, up at dawn and ready for the search, held the centre of the room; they were confident, brusque and sharp-eyed.

Outside on the steps of the house their dogs waited. It was bitterly cold and the snow was still falling; in the night it had settled knee-deep on the ground. It would, he thought, be hard to make any progress under these conditions. His mother, the neighbours agreed, had been gone for more than three hours when the snow came. If she had fallen or found shelter, it was not likely to be close by. The snow would have covered any tracks she had made and the air was probably too cold for the dogs to be able to trace any scent. Their only hope was that she had moved quickly or found company on the road and made her way with assistance to her brother's house before real darkness fell and the thick snow began to settle.

The men moved slowly, with determination. It seemed to Miquel that they knew as well as he did that this quest was pointless, that even a body would not be found under the relentless covering of snow, and that under these conditions, even reaching Coll del So would be impossible. They were doing it, he knew, because they could not do nothing, despite their dislike for his father. They would not wish it to be known that they had idled in their houses, or done easy winter work, when a woman of the village had disappeared in the snow. And so all morning they moved carefully along the road which his mother must have travelled. They stopped only when a flask of brandy and some bread and cold sausage were passed around. They did not speak much to each other but they did not speak to Miquel or his father at all.

It was well past midday, with the snow falling still, and they had not yet reached the church of Santa Magdalena where the narrow military road began. Miquel watched them consulting with each other while his father stood apart. He knew that they wished to abandon the search for the day; it would take them three hours to get back to the village. This meant that they could go forward for another hour or more and still be back before dusk, but it was clear that they were already tired, each step in the heavy snow took its toll on their energy; they would be exhausted by the time they reached home.

It was easier to dream than do anything else, to imagine his uncle driving his mother home from Pallosa after her night of rest, and his uncle's jeep appearing in the village at the same time as they all arrived back. As they turned, it struck Miquel forcefully that they all knew that his mother had not survived, that the men from the village had taken him and his father out on this vain search as a way of distracting them from the cold fact that Miquel's mother was missing, she lay dead somewhere near or below the Coll del So, covered in a metre or more of snow, that she would not ever come back to their house, unless they brought her coffin there when they found her. Walking, then, was a way of getting them used to the new fact without their having to wait all day in an empty house, with nothing happening, and nothing to say.

When they came back into the village they saw a police jeep outside their house, with two uniformed members of the Guardia Civil inside. As soon as the group of villagers came fully into view, one policeman got out of the jeep, and then, when they were closer, the one who had been in the passenger seat emerged. He was very young, Miquel noticed, and seemed almost shy. He kept his hat on as he glanced at the men coming towards him and then looked away. His companion, the driver, was middle-aged, stocky, hatless. Miquel watched him singling out his father and himself as the two men he would need to speak to and wondered how the police had been alerted. As they approached the jeep, Miquel checked the back seat in case they had found her and had her body. But there was nothing except an old rug.

His father explained, as soon as they were inside, that his wife could easily be safe, could easily have arrived in

Pallosa and be in her brother's house. The older policeman took note of the brother's name and said in a heavy southern accent that if the single telephone line to Pallosa, which was in the police station there, were back up he would call as soon as he returned to La Seu, and if the road were open would go to Pallosa. In the meantime, he needed a description of her.

As Miquel's father spoke and the policeman took notes, the younger policeman leaned against the wall, just inside the door of the kitchen, pushed his hat back on his head so Miquel was able to see his clear, unwrinkled forehead and his large dark eyes. As these eyes examined the room, seeming to concentrate briefly on the scene between the two older men, they locked with Miquel's eyes. Miquel was aware that he had been staring at the younger man since he came into the room and it would be better now if he looked away, let whatever had happened dissolve into a moment of unconcealed curiosity and nothing more. But he did not look away. He took in the young policeman's face in the shadowy light of the kitchen, the full redness of his lips, the square, hard stubbornness of his jaw and chin and then the softness of his eyes, the eyelashes like a girl's. The young policeman, in turn, watched only Miquel's eyes, his gaze cold, expressionless, as though he were sullenly blaming him for something. When Miquel looked down at the policeman's crotch, he too glanced down at himself and he briefly smiled, opening his lips, before resuming his former expression, but more intense now, almost feral, staking out an object within his grasp.

As his colleague finished taking his notes and appeared ready to depart, the younger policeman took off his hat. Miquel, across the room, quietly acknowledged the gesture. Then the young policeman, who had not spoken once, turned and opened the door, allowing his colleague to leave first, gesturing to Miquel's father to follow, trying, it seemed to Miquel, to engineer a moment when the two older men would be outside and the two younger ones at the door, or inside the hall. But Miquel's father held back, insisting, out of politeness, that the younger policeman should go out before him. Miquel watched the younger policeman carefully as his companion reversed the jeep and turned and slowed for a second before driving away.

As Miquel busied himself doing his mother's tasks, his father went outside and began to chop wood, striking frantic blows with the hatchet, splitting blocks of wood they could have easily burned in one piece. Miquel dreaded the night, when they would have nothing left to do but wait for news of her, knowing that it might not come soon.

He remembered a game he had begun to play with her as soon as he could walk. He did not know how it had started, but, with her in the room, he used to hide under the table, or under the bed, or behind a chair, and she then would pretend that she could not find him, and they would both let it continue until the moment before he became scared. Then he would appear and she would feign surprise and shock and delight, and lift him up in the air. He had no memory of ever doing this while his father was present and, once Jordi could understand things, he would grow frightened by the disappearance and the mock search and was made jealous by his mother's and his brother's shouts of recognition and sudden greeting. As Miquel moved around the house now, he was acutely alert to the shadowy places, becoming darker in the twilight, the places where you could hide and then appear, as though his mother might mysteriously arrive and position herself where she could not be instantly found.

That evening they ate in silence some more fried eggs and stale bread and cold sausage until Miquel asked their father what they should do about Jordi. Even though they had no address for him, no idea where he was, they could ask the police in La Seu to make contact with him.

'And say what?' his father asked.

Miquel did not answer him.

'He has enough to worry about,' his father said.

'He might hear it from someone.'

'He's well out of earshot.'

'You can meet people from home,' Miquel said. 'You never know who you are going to meet, and they could have heard the news.'

'For the moment,' his father said, 'we'll tell him nothing, we'll leave him in peace.'

When they had eaten, Foix, who had made himself the leader of the search all that day, called to the door but refused to come in, even though it was snowing hard outside. The phone lines, he said, were still down. His brother-in-law, he added, had made it through to the village and left behind two dogs who were trained to follow a scent. He had worked with them before, he said, and they were the best. So they would set out with the dogs at first light, all the men who had been with them would come again, even though the terrain might be more difficult because there could be a bigger fall of snow during the night.

Before they went to bed, his father told him that he was going to try to drive the jeep to La Seu the next day and then across the paved road to Sort and then, if he could, to Pallosa. Miquel said that he would go with the men, but when he went to the window and looked out and saw the snow coming down even thicker than before, he realized that neither his father nor the men would go very far the next day, and the village could, if the snow continued to fall as it was falling now, be cut off on both sides.

His father and himself, Miquel realized, were sleeping alone in rooms where the stark absences were palpable; it was hard to remember that both his mother and Jordi were gone, and that should Jordi return and she should not, then her absence would seem even greater. He lay on Jordi's bed for a while until the cold made him undress and seek refuge under his own blankets. He wished it were two weeks earlier, before Jordi had left; he wished it were three years earlier, when he had just come home; he wished it were any time but now.

In the morning again he was woken by feet on the floorboards in the room below; he had slept deeply, and he longed for more time in the oblivion from which he had just been snatched. Instantly, he knew he would have to rise and spend the day searching for his mother in the freezing air, the snow getting into his boots; his toes, like his fingers, would be utterly frozen. He looked at Jordi's bed and wondered if he concentrated hard enough could he get in touch with him to reassure him that they were all well, despite the winter, and that he had no news to tell, nothing had happened since Jordi left.

Foix, when Miquel appeared in the kitchen, took him aside and said that the two dogs, waiting outside, would need a scent to work from, and the better the scent the better the chance of finding her. Thus he would, he said, need something that belonged to her, something she wore. He began to whisper as he told Miquel that her clothes, if they had been washed since she had last worn them, would not be of much use; the closer to her body the garment had been worn the more useful it would be. He looked at Miquel as though they were both conspirators against not only everyone in the room, but against the snow-covered world outside as well.

Miquel's father, sure now that he would not get his jeep up the steep hill beyond the curve out of the village on the road to La Seu, was sitting alone at the table as more men came and more dogs yelped in the freezing morning. The snow had stopped in the night; before the dawn the temperature had dropped which meant they had to watch for patches of ice as well as deep snow. His father seemed forlorn, exhausted, distant from what was happening around him. Miquel decided not to trouble him about Foix's request, to go upstairs alone and try to find something of his mother's which had preserved her scent.

He had forgotten how well he knew the chest of drawers

under the window of his parents' bedroom. He had not been near it for years, but when he was a small boy his favourite pastime, under his mother's supervision, was opening each drawer and taking out the contents and then folding them and replacing them exactly as he had found them. In the top drawer she kept documents and bills and receipts on one side and handkerchiefs and scarves on the other. The middle drawer was where she kept her blouses and cardigans, and in the two bottom drawers she kept her underwear. When she opened these drawers the smell was not of her, but of lavender and perfume. He did not touch anything; nothing here would be any use to Foix and his dogs.

In a corner of the room was the old basket, the same size as the one in his own room, where dirty clothes were thrown. It was only half-full; on the top were shirts his father had worn with some socks and shorts and vests, and at the very bottom were the last things his mother had worn in this house and left here, as well as the blouse she had worn on the night of Jordi's dinner which, he imagined, she was keeping so she could wash it and dry it in some special way. Below this was some of her underwear which he took and held, and then, checking that no one was behind him, he lifted to his nose. He buried his face in the intimate smell of her, which was clear despite the days that had passed since she had worn this underwear. It carried a sharp hint of her into this cold room and, for a moment, he imagined the dogs moving blindly through the landscape, living only with this smell, seeking its loving source under the snow or in the undergrowth. He would walk behind them. He dropped all of the undergarments except one back into the basket, tucking them under his father's clothes, and carried the one he had selected downstairs and gave it to Foix, who was waiting with the dogs outside the door.

The day was much colder than the one before and progress was much harder as the two new dogs followed phantom scents which led them off the road and high into the hills while the men had to wait for them below. Miquel's father followed them far behind most of the time, giving no impression that he was searching for her or looking for clues as to where she might be. Miquel noticed

Foix and Castellet and some of the other men glancing back at him, clearly irritated. He noticed also that their neighbours, on this second day's searching, were more animated, seemed to enjoy shouting at the dogs, had more life in them the more time went on. Their very excitement caused his father to appear uninterested, almost bored as he trudged behind them as though his only aim were not to wet his feet.

The two dogs, Miquel thought, had more energy than intelligence, and he wondered why Foix did not realize, as he did now, that anything buried under a mound of freezing snow would be unlikely to yield a scent. But he knew that there was nothing else he could do except move forward in what was, with the exception of fox and wild-boar tracks, a flat, virgin whiteness, seeming innocent, almost beautiful, utterly harmless, its treacherous nature lying in layers under its blank surface.

By early afternoon they could go no further; the snow was too deep, and it was becoming hard to tell where the road ahead began to dip and rise and where the margin was and how steep the fall. The dogs, who had not been fed since early morning, were increasingly difficult; two of them from the village began a vicious fight, snarling and yelping as they tore at each other, having to be held by their owners, and then kicked into surly submission. Miquel noticed that all the men took part in separating them and holding them and shouting at them except himself and his father, who stood back watching, and he felt that this, too, annoyed the men. Thus he was glad when they gave up the search, having to wait for the two new dogs to come back from whatever vain quest they had been on, and began to make their way back. Miquel was careful to walk with the other men, stay between two of them, or close to one. His father lagged so far behind that several times when he turned his head he could not see him.

That night his father insisted that there would be no more futile outings, that these men hated him and had spent two days uselessly walking the road merely as a way of torturing him and humiliating him. He would have no more of them, he said. In the morning, he said, they would go to La Seu, where it would be market day, whether the road was open or not; they would drive to the point where it was closed and wait there, or wade through whatever snow was blocking the road.

Miquel, without consulting his father, left the house and called on Foix, who, when he came to the door, asked him almost aggressively what he wanted. Miquel told him that they would not be searching the next day, but going to La Seu, where they might meet people from Pallosa. They could also speak to the police. He added that he wished to thank Foix for all his help.

'And your father?' Foix asked. 'We all know he has a tongue. Has he lost the use of it?'

Miquel held his gaze calmly.

'He is very upset.'

Foix closed the door without speaking. When Miquel went home, he did not tell his father where he had been.

The road to La Seu was open, but icy in stretches, dangerously so in the early morning. Miquel had slept a dreamless sleep and for the first few minutes of the day had believed that this would be another normal day in his life. The night had erased all memory of the days just passed. But his father, he saw when he went downstairs, had not slept at all, seemed worn out, stopping halfway through every sentence, having forgotten what it was he had wanted to say. His father's sleepless state appeared to make him drive more cautiously, keep his speed down on bends and slopes. There was almost no traffic on the road. Even the main road, when they reached it, was quiet and this was unusual for a market day.

Two weeks before this he had walked here with his mother, stood in the queue with her, noticed her snatching time from him to down three drinks, and now he and his father moved through the early hours of the market, as the stalls were barely set up, in search of someone from Pallosa or Burch or Tirvia, or any of the other villages around, who might have news of her. Miquel knew it was most likely that, because of the bad roads and the broken phone lines, no one would know anything about her, and they would have to be told, as though it were a guilty secret, what had happened, and then news would begin to spread. He thought of suggesting to his father that, instead of walking all morning through the ghostly market, they should find out if the road to Pallosa were open and go

there now, consult his uncle before his uncle heard it as a
rumour or a half-digested piece of news from someone else.

They had a bocadillo in a bar. Both of them were raven-
ously hungry; Miquel was tempted when he was finished
to say that he wanted another. He was determined to buy
some food as they had been living on the eggs collected
from the hens and little else for three days now. But, since
his father wanted to go to the police station, he thought
he would wait, have a coffee now, and eat more later,
perhaps even a proper lunch. They walked past the stalls
in the direction of the police station, careful to look at
none of the vendors and greet none of them, since they
did not wish stall-holders, who might have heard about
the missing woman, to ask them about her. But they were
still watching for people from the villages around Pallosa.

As they turned into one of the side streets, having passed
the bread shop, they saw Francesc, Miquel's uncle, his
mother's brother from Pallosa, coming towards them, with
his wife and a neighbouring woman. Miquel stopped
immediately and let his father go forward to meet them.
He stood in a doorway as he watched his father greeting

63

them. He could see his uncle's and aunt's faces but he could not tell, at first, anything by their expressions. His uncle merely nodded, his aunt and the neighbour listened intently. Slowly, however, he noticed his uncle's face darkening; it was a small change, he did not wrinkle his brow or move his mouth, but it was enough for Miquel. He knew even before his uncle spoke and shook his head and his aunt put her hand over her mouth and the other woman moved to console her, he knew that his mother had not arrived safely in Pallosa, and, from the way his uncle now seemed to question his father, he knew that his uncle and aunt had not been aware of his mother's disappearance. He moved out of the shadows and made his way towards them.

The road to Pallosa had been cut off for two days, his uncle said, and the single telephone line had been down. As Miquel watched him, his uncle appeared to be having trouble breathing, he was taking heavy breaths between his words, staring at the ground, his brow all wrinkled now.

'And that day, the snow came down,' he said, 'faster than anyone can remember. We were up to our necks in it.'

Miquel could see his uncle holding back a fundamental question as he discovered what time she had left at, who had seen her, how long she had been walking before the snow came. His uncle, it was obvious, wished to know why she had left, how they did not notice her leaving, how they did not know at what time she had taken off on such a dangerous journey, and why she was walking when there was, if she needed to go to Pallosa, a jeep outside the door. As his uncle searched their eyes, Miquel became aware of his slow realization that she had left in distress, or after an argument, and, he thought, the more his uncle seemed quietly to make a judgement, the more guilty his father and he must have appeared.

They decided that they should walk to the police station together and declare her officially a missing person. His uncle believed that the police would then be obliged to look for her, using all their resources. His uncle, he knew, had a reputation for kindness and intelligence and, as Miquel watched him taking control, he remembered his mother's lamenting that there was no one like Francesc in their village, to whom you could go if you had a problem.

Close to the police station, out of the corner of his eye and then very clearly, Miquel saw Foix and Castellet standing behind a jeep in the company of two policemen. His uncle saw them too, but Miquel realized that he did not recognize them; his father looked only at the ground and Miquel did not draw his attention to the presence of the villagers in La Seu.

The policeman at the desk appeared to know about the case and told them that they would have to wait. There were only two chairs in the narrow hallway. All five of them, in turn, refused to sit down and they made an awkward grouping as policemen passed in and out, forcing them to move out of the way and stand aside. Eventually, Miquel's aunt and her companion said they would go back to the market and meet later at the cafe beside the bread shop. Miquel said that he would go with them; he needed to buy supplies in the market. It might be easier, he thought, for his father to tell his uncle what had really happened if he were not listening. He noticed before he left how handsome his uncle was and how bright and alert he seemed as he waited in the hall. Beside him, his father looked like a poor man from a poor village, humble and uneasy in the official building in the big town.

They walked towards the market. He knew by the way his aunt was speaking to her neighbour, arranging to separate from her briefly, that she wanted to be alone with him, and he presumed that she wanted to know what had happened. She did not have her husband's patient ability to fathom something in full without having to be furnished with all the details. Miquel could see, her friend having departed, that she was angling now for a complete account of his mother's last hours in the house. He decided, without knowing why, that he would not tell her.

When she asked him if he would come with her to the butcher's, he realized that she meant to go to the one his mother frequented, and he was not ready for the idea that they would remember him, the young man whose brother was going to the mili, and ask about his mother. He would have no idea what to say. The dream in which he was now partaking, a world of queues and shoppers and market stalls, seemed by its very vividness to preclude the possibility that the darkness of the previous few days could have any meaning, could even be mentioned. He told his aunt that he did not want to go into the butcher's shop with her, but would meet her later as arranged with his father and uncle.

'What happened?' she asked as they stood outside the shop.

'We don't know,' he said. 'She walked out of the village towards Pallosa.'

His aunt sighed in exasperation.

'Is that all that happened?' Her gaze was sharp and accusatory. 'She just walked out for no reason on a freezing winter's day?'

He nodded.

'Well, she didn't arrive,' his aunt said.

'I don't know what we are going to do without her,' Miquel replied.

He knew that he had now cut off any further questions from his aunt, but saying it, allowing the note of sadness which he had struck merely as a strategy to prevent her from continuing, had had its own effect on him, and he found that he had begun to cry. He turned and walked away from her, his hand over his face so that no one could see his tears, and he did not look back.

Later, when he came to the cafe, his father and uncle had not arrived. His aunt greeted him coldly. He ordered a sandwich and had to concentrate hard, when it came, not to grab it and eat it in a few bites. When he had eaten it, he felt once more a desperate need to order another one.

When his aunt's friend appeared and sat down, she examined him curiously.

'I could not believe it when I saw you earlier,' she said. 'You look the image of your grandfather from Pallosa, it's more than that, every single thing about you is like him. I mean even the way you are looking at me now.'

'He was old when I knew him,' his aunt joined in, 'but I remember them all saying it. Even when you were small you did things that reminded your mother of him.'

'I never met him,' Miquel said.

'Well, it's like meeting a ghost,' the woman said.

'She never mentioned it,' Miquel said.

'I wish my husband was here,' the woman went on. 'He

would be amazed by you, even the way you are looking away from me now, he'd be amazed.'

'I suppose we all look like people in our families,' his aunt said. 'I suppose it's natural.'

It was clear to Miquel when his father and his uncle finally arrived that they had walked from the police station in silence. Miquel sensed also that his father had been asked questions which had deeply unsettled him. He could look at none of them as he sat down.

His uncle then explained that the police would set in train a professional search, working from both villages, the one she walked out of and the one to which she was bound. They saw no reason why the family or the villagers should join them, it would be a nuisance, he said. It would begin in the morning at first light as, in his opinion, it should have begun two days earlier. But there was nothing could be done, he said, except hope that this search would yield results. Miquel almost smiled at the thought that his uncle was speaking like a policeman.

When he and his father got home after a slow journey on the icy roads, the jeep stalling and slipping on each slope, and sliding dangerously on a number of curves, night had almost fallen. At first he did not recognize the three jeeps parked in front of their house. Everything that was happening had such newness to it that three strange jeeps meant nothing, were hardly worthy of comment. Then he saw that they were police jeeps and that there were two policemen standing at the door watching their arrival closely, having recognized them, and having, he surmised, been waiting for their return. He had not seen either of these policemen before. They nodded in acknowledgement but did not speak as they approached them. They let them pass into the house. In the kitchen, the young policeman who had come the day after her disappearance was already sitting on a chair near the window. He did not change his blank expression when Miquel turned on the electric light in the room.

When the older policeman who had been in their house before came downstairs, he announced that the police were searching the house and the barns below. They could hear the sounds of heavy boots on the floorboards of the rooms upstairs. Miquel moved to go up, but the older one barred his way.

'No, no,' he said. 'Both of you please stay down here.'

'What do you think you are going to find up there?' his father asked.

'Both of you stay down here,' the policeman repeated and nodded in the direction of the younger policeman, who stood up as if to guard the way. Miquel noticed that his eyes were duller than the last time, his hair less shiny. He responded to Miquel's gaze with pure equanimity, gazing back without seeming to heed in the slightest way what he saw. He did not once look at Miquel's father, who had taken a chair and was sitting at the kitchen table.

As the older policeman left the house, they heard a noise coming from one of the barns; one of the big old doors, Miquel guessed, was being pulled back. He moved towards the window so that he could see what was happening, but quietly the young policeman motioned to him without speaking that he must stay where he was.

'Are we under arrest?' Miquel's father asked.

The policeman did not look at him and did not answer. He kept his eyes on Miquel and then on his father; his look had no hostility in it, it was powerful merely because

72

it was relentlessly vacant. His face in its wilful immobility resembled a heavy white mask. He had not yet spoken to them; his voice, his accent, would tell them too much about him. Being prevented from going to the window did not worry Miquel; he knew they were not under arrest, that the search of the house and barns was a routine matter, encouraged perhaps by Foix and Castellet. The young policeman had kept him from moving, he believed, out of timidity, a fear of his superiors rather than any authority of his own. As the three of them remained there, his father slumped in his chair staring at the ground, Miquel and the policeman locked eyes and then looked away, glancing at each other again after a while, Miquel running his eyes over the young man's body. The policeman watched him doing this with something between acceptance and indifference until Miquel stood up and went again to the window. The policeman shrugged but did not move.

Miquel could see that the seven or eight policemen now gathered in front of the house had been joined by Foix and Castellet. He could not tell, however, from what direction they had come, if they had been in the barns as well. Their everyday clothes did nothing to undermine the authority they seemed to have among the policemen, who were all outsiders. They were listening closely now as Foix spoke and made gestures. Miquel's father came to the window and watched them too, but since he had not noticed them in La Seu, Miquel realized that he would fail to grasp the significance of their standing with the police outside the door. Miquel wondered what they had said to place themselves in such a position of apparent trust. When the young policeman was finally called to join the others, he left the house without speaking, and the three jeeps drove away, leaving Foix and Castellet to walk slowly up the village in the snow.

He and his father were alone now. Miquel did not think that any of their neighbours would come near them; they would not be needed in the search of the mountain which the police would conduct. Again, he thought that they should write to Jordi, but the letter would now have to say what he and his father had failed even to say to each other. He knew that Jordi, if he received such a letter, would have to come home, whether he got permission or not. But even if he did get permission, it would only be for a few days. Miquel imagined him arriving to find nothing, an emptiness in the house, his father reduced to silence, with nothing to do, no grave to visit, no body to touch, no coffin to carry, no words of consolation from those around. Instead, a frozen landscape and the dreaded days with no thaw.

Miquel could not visualize Jordi's response to a letter, he tried to picture him reading it and then moving fast from wherever he was towards them. All his life, from the time he was a small child, an injured cat or a limping dog or any sort of hungry animal would cause Jordi to panic. All through his childhood they had to prevent him from befriending stray dogs or neighbours' cats. He had to be kept indoors when the hunters were in the forest shooting the wild boars and then dragging them bloody through the village. Away, he would miss Clua, whom Miquel and his father hardly tolerated, as much as he missed any of them. The idea that his mother might be missing or in danger would be unbearable to him; the fact that she was gone, buried deep in snow somewhere in the distance, could not be conveyed to him now. And yet Miquel also understood that not telling him, leaving him to live as though this event had not occurred, was a real piece of treachery.

As they were eating, a knock came to the door which made them look up at one another in fright. When Miquel answered, he saw Josep Bernat with a parcel in his hand. Bernat had come on the two days' search, but he had remained in the background so that he was hardly noticed. He said he would not come in, but his wife had made bread and there were some other things from her larder in the bag that he hoped they would find useful. He bowed to them and departed as soon as Miquel had thanked him.

Bernat began to call in the evenings, often bringing a can of milk or some fresh produce with him, almost as an excuse to visit. Since Miquel had started to go out alone, sometimes beyond Santa Magdalena to venture along the military road where the snow had hardened in the freezing temperatures and each step had to be taken with care, Bernat was full of advice and ideas about where he should look. He seemed to know about every death in the area since the Civil War, especially suicides and accidental deaths. La Senyora Fluvia, whose husband was still alive, who had fallen in the snow a dozen years back, was a favourite subject of Bernat's. Her family, he said, had passed where she was lying every day for two months but she was covered in a patch of ice on which the sun never shone and thus she lay there until there was a general thaw. Or that man who was married to the Englishwoman, who was a painter – and he drove his jeep off the road near Pallosa and killed a child as well.

'It's a pity,' he said one night, 'that you did not get through with the jeep that first day, you might have found her.'

Miquel's father nodded.

Miquel was interested in Bernat's real opinion about where his mother was and when or how she might be found, but he could never get direct answers. On the nights when Bernat came to the house, Miquel listened to his stories and then tried to turn the conversation to the possibility of a sudden thaw being the most dangerous for her, because her body would still not be easily found, but she would be open to birds and animals before they could get to her. Bernat agreed and thought for a while and waited until Miquel's father had left the room and told him that, since the police had not found her and they had looked closely, then in his opinion her body would not be located until the spring thaw, until there was no snow or ice at all on that stretch of land. And then they would have to watch the sky all day, he said, and if they saw vultures they would have to get into the jeep and race towards whatever it was the vultures were circling. And that is, he said, how you will find her.

4

Neither of them could cook. His father refused to try but did not stop complaining about the monotony of the food. Too many eggs, he said. Too much cold ham. Miquel tried to cook rice but it came out grainy and hard, he did not know if had put in too little water or too much. The potatoes he boiled seemed to dissolve in the water. They depended on Bernat for bread. He did not know how his mother had found the meat for stews and could offer a variety of dishes with no shop or supplier in the village. When he tried to cook lentils, his father tipped the plate, full of hot food, into the bucket where food for the hens was kept.

Slowly, the hens began to lay fewer eggs, and gradually

the rabbits began to die. Miquel knew that he had neglected them in the early days of his mother's disappearance, but, even though he had quickly established a routine of feeding both the hens and the rabbits, they did not thrive. He spent a day cleaning out the hen house, presuming that the accumulated dirt had caused them to lay fewer eggs, but when he found egg shells everywhere among the dirt, it caused him to wonder if the hens were not, in fact, eating the very eggs they laid. He wished there were someone in the village whom he could approach and ask, but he knew his father would object even if he were to mention his difficulty to Bernat.

As the rabbits died, he thought it strange how contented the other rabbits seemed, how normally they behaved, even though one of them lay dead in their cage, its body all stiff and useless, its eyes staring at some vague distant point. It was good for nothing now, he quietly buried it behind the barn. He did not want his father to know that he was having any domestic problems beyond the ones which were obvious.

After a time, only the big brown rabbits were still alive; they seemed to grow fatter and healthier the more white rabbits died. Miquel kept their cages clean while his father paid them no attention. In these days in the hen house he was lucky if he found even one egg in the morning. His father, he thought, must have presumed that he was not served eggs because he was tired of them. Nothing his father ate pleased him. He took to eating cured ham and bread softened with tomato and oil, and doing so not at mealtimes but when he felt hungry. He did not eat the crusts of the bread but left them on the table for Miquel to give to Clua.

One day he came into the kitchen as Miquel was eating a sausage with beans, which Bernat's wife had left him.

'I'm going to La Seu tomorrow,' he said. 'I thought I'd take a few rabbits to sell and some eggs.'

Miquel glanced up at him nervously.

'The rabbits are dying. I don't know how to keep them alive. The hens have stopped laying.'

'What did you do to them?' his father asked.

'I'm not a woman. I don't know anything about them.'

'You're no housekeeper,' his father said and laughed faintly to himself. 'Do you know that?'

'Why don't you look after them yourself?' Miquel asked.

'No, I won't be doing that,' his father replied. 'Dead rabbits! Does anyone in the village know?'

'No.'

'That's good. And we have no eggs?'

'There's one in the bowl on the shelf.'

'We should keep it as a souvenir.'

Miquel did not go to La Seu with his father; the sky had cleared two days in a row, which meant that some of the snow had melted. He took his binoculars and set out early with the intention of reaching Santa Magdalena well before noon and then seeing how far he could make it along the military road, some of which he knew was still deep in snow. Once he was in the sun, he was warm, at times too warm so that he had to remove his coat. For an hour or so he trudged along the narrow road. Knowing that he was free of his father's company and the empty shadowy bareness of the house, which bore the marks of his mother's absence in every corner and on every surface, made him almost happy. The only dread was having to turn back eventually, finding the limits which the banked-up snow had created. The road as far as Santa Magdalena was, he discovered, much clearer than anyone in the village had said. In some places the thaw had been complete and he scanned it with the binoculars in case there was any sign. It struck him how unlucky his mother had been in the hour she chose to make her desperate flight from them, and the day on which she had gone. Had she left an hour earlier, she would, he thought, have reached Pallosa safely, and had she departed an hour later, she would have got no further than here, and known to turn back. She was caught, he believed, in the very wrong hour and she lay somewhere beneath a mound of snow in the slopes below the military road which he scanned as well, seeing nothing beyond the whiteness except stumps of trees.

It was strange, he thought, that hardly any melting of snow had happened on the military road. Much of it received the same sunlight as the road on which he had just walked. But the military road was open to the wind, was cut sharply into the mountain with no trees or under-growth on either side. If the wind blew snow from most directions, it would bank up on the road, which was a groove made by outsiders quickly into the earth without any thought for the terrain or knowledge of what would happen in the winter. Soon he found that the snow was up to his knees and that each step required an effort and then a further effort to extricate himself.

He turned back and trudged through the slush for miles until he came to the village. He wished his father would learn to do something in the house, even learn how to light the fire. He would come back from La Seu, Miquel knew, with too many provisions or too few, with kilos of meat they could not keep fresh, or enough sausages for just one meal.

His father was not home, which was surprising as he had left early in the morning and had nothing much to do there. Perhaps he went and saw the police again but, as far as Miquel could see, there was no point in that. There was no bread; he fried some potatoes and the egg his father wished to keep as a souvenir and he lit a fire. In these days, when he thought about his mother the feelings were sharpened by guilt, a gnawing presence in his chest which he could obliterate only by deliberately thinking about something else but which could easily and stealthily return. He regretted now that he had never, in recent years, come in like this to her kitchen on an ordinary day and watched her cooking or lighting the fire and offered to help her, or keep her company while she worked. He also knew that he should have been braver the day before she disappeared, he should have gone to her and told her that he himself would replace what his father had thrown out. He should, he thought, have forced his father not to leave her alone in a room craving alcohol. He knew that if he had been brave, he could have prevented her from leaving.

It was late when he heard the jeep pulling up in front of the house. He had spent the evening looking into the fire, dreaming half the time of leaving there, going as suddenly as his mother did, but towards La Seu and then towards Lérida or Barcelona, or even further away, and never appearing again. Not ever seeing his brother, would, he thought, be a high price to pay for the new freedom he would win, but maybe they could meet elsewhere, maybe Jordi would leave too. And the rest of the time he entertained all the guilt that wished to call, carried in by the wind through the darkness, to enter his spirit as he pondered over and over his own responsibility for her disappearance and her death.

He heard voices outside and thought it odd that his father had given a lift to someone from the village. Perhaps Bernat, with whom his father seemed on better terms each day, had travelled back from La Seu with him or had been collected from some other place. As he heard footsteps cutting into the brittle sheet of ice on the path outside the house, he did not move. If his father needed help to carry goods from the jeep, he could come and ask him. His father, when he walked into the kitchen, smiled at him benevolently, warmly. He was carrying bags. Behind him appeared a pale young man, smaller in height than Miquel, but strong-looking and not yet twenty, he thought. He, too, was carrying bags. Miquel was sure that he had never seen him before. He glanced towards Miquel but did not smile. Miquel turned his attention to the fire as though he were alone, taking two blocks of wood from the basket and placing them strategically in the grate.

'We're hungry,' his father said. 'We haven't eaten. Manolo here will make the supper.'

Manolo turned towards Miquel, who stoked the fire casually and said nothing.

'I had my supper,' Miquel said, 'but I could do with some more.'

Manolo's eyes were dark, his hair jet black. He began to open cupboards, checking the contents and then storing any packages from the bags they had carried from the jeep.

As they ate a supper of sausages, beans and fresh bread, it emerged that Miquel's father had met neighbours of his brother-in-law from Pallosa to whom he had explained his plight. He needed someone to keep house for them, he said, but he did not think anyone could be found as they had no room for a girl or woman to sleep in, and there was no neighbouring woman available. The people from Pallosa had told him that Manolo, who was an orphan, was free; he worked for local farms in the spring and summer and lived with them, but in the winter there was less to do. Not only would he welcome housework, they said, which he could do very well, but the people with whom he was now lodged would welcome a mouth less to feed. Miquel's father had decided, he said, to drive to Pallosa there and then and find Manolo and his employer, who had agreed to release him immediately.

'And so I bundled him into the jeep,' his father said. 'He says he can cook and we'll soon find out.'

His father smiled conspiratorially at Manolo, who did not respond but gazed gravely at Miquel, to whom it was clear that that his father's account of finding Manolo was like a story of buying an animal or a sack of rice. Manolo, it seemed to Miquel, realized this too, and became openly downcast the more his father, full of good humour, spoke.

As they were sitting at the table eating, Miquel realized that he himself had not spoken much and wondered if his silence was further disheartening the new arrival.

'My father is a monster,' he said. 'You've made a big mistake coming with him.'

He and his father began to laugh, but the boy remained silent, appearing to become even sadder the more they laughed. As soon as they had finished eating, he began to clear off the table; he put a pan of water on to boil and started to stack dishes, which had been left for days, to wash. Miquel moved back to his position by the fire while his father stayed at the table.

'Are there bedclothes anywhere?' his father asked.

Miquel shrugged. They had not changed the sheets since his mother left. He did not know if the sheets stored in the cupboard would need to be aired by the fire before they were used.

'Anyway,' his father said, 'the mattress on Jordi's bed will be well aired.'

'Why don't we move it down to the store room?' Miquel asked.

'The window is broken there,' his father said. 'He'll freeze.'

'I don't want him in my room,' Miquel said.

Manolo, who had his back to them, stopped moving. He made no effort to pretend that he was not listening.

'We'll put him there tonight,' his father said. 'And I'll show him where the sheets and blankets are, so he can make his own bed.'

Miquel sighed and stared into the fire. When he looked up again, Manolo had resumed his work at the stove and the sink. When he moved across the room to clean the table he did not look at Miquel. By the time Miquel went to his bedroom, his father had already shown Manolo the way, and helped him carry sheets and blankets and a pillow to the room, which seemed almost cramped when Miquel entered it. Manolo was studiously unfolding each blanket and then spreading it meticulously across the bed. He did not turn when Miquel came in, only when the door was closed. He did not greet him, but continued to work as Miquel stood and watched him, waiting until he was finished before getting undressed.

Manolo rummaged in a small suitcase as Miquel lay in bed. This was, as far as he could make out, the only bag Manolo had brought with him. It had barely space for a change of clothes. When Manolo took off his pullover, Miquel saw that his shirt was torn at the back and frayed at the cuffs and collar. Downstairs, he had noticed a smell, like something rotting, which became more intense when

Manolo took off his shoes. It was only when Manolo had removed his trousers and was putting them over a chair that Miquel realized the smell came from the boy's socks, which he now began to remove. He put them on the floor under his bed and looked at Miquel for permission to turn off the light.

'Can you leave your shoes and socks outside the door?' Miquel asked.

Manolo nodded, showing no sign that he had any objection to doing this. As he bent to collect his socks and then moved across the room to pick up his shoes, Miquel realized that he had brought no pyjamas with him and that he was not wearing any shorts. He was going to sleep wearing his old shirt. When he had put the shoes and socks outside, and closed the door, he turned off the light and crossed the room. Neither of them spoke as they lay in the dark. Miquel guessed that Manolo fell quickly asleep.

He imagined writing to Jordi now with the news. Our mother has disappeared, she is dead, lying encased in ice, we will have to watch the sky for vultures when the thaw comes so that we can find her before they do. Your bed is being slept in by a dark, silent, sad-looking boy who has arrived without many clothes and seems willing to do a woman's work. He has moved in beside me, I can hear his breathing, which is light and regular. In the morning, I will try and find another place for him to sleep.

5

He walked each day as far as he could; the snow was starting to melt along the military road and some stretches of the road to Santa Magdalena were dry. He walked each day at a different time, depending on the work he had to do, but he could often leave his father and Manolo to manage. His father, by this time, had begun to work cutting stones for Josep Bernat and spent some time away from his own house. Manolo worked hard, cooking and washing and cleaning and helping with the animals if he were needed.

As the thaw continued, Miquel's uncle came from Pallosa, and drove his jeep along the road out of the village as far as Santa Magdalena and then walked with Miquel along the military road, most of which now was clear, even though the land around it was deep in snow. He got out of the jeep several times and surveyed the landscape with Miquel's binoculars. When Miquel told him what Bernat had said about the vultures, he agreed. They would have to wait, he said, and watch for them, and hope to find her as soon as the temperature rose. He did not think, he said, that any vultures had appeared over Pallosa yet, nor anywhere higher than Sort. If he saw them hovering, then he would know that the real spring had begun.

When he came face to face with Manolo in the house, Francesc embraced him and greeted him warmly. Miquel stood back as Manolo smiled and asked about people and events in Pallosa; he was more animated than he had been since he came to their house.

Outside, before he left, his uncle told him that Manolo's father had been taken into custody and shot at the end of the war when his mother was still pregnant. His mother had lived only for another year, dying of tuberculosis, but dying too, he thought, because of the loss. Manolo was brought up by his father's cousins until he could work and then moved to various houses around Pallosa, some of whom treated him badly. It was a very sad story, his uncle said, because Manolo's father had been hardly involved in the war at all, he was just unlucky. He hoped Manolo would be happier here than he had been in some other quarters. Miquel knew by the way his uncle spoke that it was obvious that he and Manolo had not become friends. That evening, Manolo seemed grateful and surprised when he was given some of Jordi's clothes by Miquel, some shirts and shorts and a pair of old boots. He promised that he would look after them carefully.

The weather grew worse; fresh snow fell and there were two days and nights of wind which blew the surface snow into the air and whirled it about as though it were dust. Miquel's father disappeared to Bernat's barn as soon as he and Miquel had taken care of the animals. He returned for lunch and then left again. His new work seemed to make him happy; he was full of jokes and good cheer as soon as he sat down at the table.

In the days when Miquel could not work outside because of the weather, he remained in the kitchen, and tried to talk to Manolo about where he had learned to cook, and how he was feeding the hens, but the replies were merely polite and restrained. It was clear that Manolo did not want to talk. He worked quietly, moving about the house, his expression solemn, dutiful. Slowly, under his care, they began to have eggs from the hens again and the rabbits began to thrive. Despite their invitation, he did not eat with them, but ate standing at the stove, usually beginning when they had finished. And despite Miquel's telling him that he did not need to do so, he placed his shoes and socks outside the bedroom door each night before he turned off the light. He made sure that Clua was fed, but several times Miquel noticed him stopping the dog following him or jumping up on him affectionately.

Miquel's father joked with Manolo that he would make a great wife for a man; all Manolo would need was a skirt, his father said, and he could travel to all the festas in the summer and by the autumn he would be walking down the aisle. Manolo never smiled when this, or one of the many varieties of it, was said, but continued whatever he was doing. Slowly, it became one of Miquel's father's constant themes.

'Oh, we'll have to get a skirt for you,' he would say. 'You're the best housewife in the whole country. Better than any young girl of your age. You know, I think they might have sent us a girl. Maybe you're only pretending to be a boy.'

One day, when these comments had been made more than once in the course of a meal and had begun to sound like taunts, Manolo approached the table and stood in front of Miquel's father.

'If you say that again, I will leave.'

His father pushed his chair back and gazed up at Manolo, who had grown much paler than usual.

'I didn't mean . . .' his father began.

'I know what you meant,' Manolo said. 'And if you say it again, I will leave.'

'I didn't mean to offend you.'

'Don't say it again, then.'

'You've become very cheeky, haven't you?' Miquel's father said.

Manolo returned to the stove and kept his back to them. Miquel watched his father battling with his own face, trying to find a way to make a joke of this, and realizing, it seemed to Miquel, that Manolo had left him no opening.

'Are you not happy here?' his father asked Manolo, who did not turn or speak.

'I'm asking you a question,' his father said.

'Stop saying I'm a girl,' Manolo said without turning.

'I never actually said you were a girl. When did I say you were a girl? When did I actually say that?' his father said.

Manolo did not respond.

'Are you deaf?' his father asked. 'When did I say you were a girl?'

Miquel could see Manolo's shoulders hunching as though he were going to cry. His own feeling of powerlessness, his not finding a way to intervene, brought back to him the scene on the day before his mother had left. As his father stood up, he realized that he could not allow this cruel version of the earlier event to continue.

'Leave him alone,' he said to his father, 'and sit down!'

His father, he knew, would have no idea how to behave now. Miquel had been on the point of adding that his father had already caused enough trouble in the house, but was happy that he had restrained himself. His father stood with his eyes on the floor as Manolo crossed the room and gathered plates as though nothing had happened. Miquel did not move and made sure that his father could not even hear his breathing. He tried to do nothing. In the end, having heaved a long sigh, his father left the kitchen and returned to his work at Bernat's. Miquel smiled at Manolo when he returned to the table. The smile Manolo managed in return was all the more powerful for being half-hidden and quick to disappear.

For the first time that night Manolo spoke to Miquel in the bedroom. Having left his shoes and socks outside the door, he turned off the light and crossed the room and got into bed.

'The winds won't keep up like this,' he said.

'It's getting worse every day,' Miquel replied.

'You often cry in the night,' Manolo said. 'It's not loud or anything, but I hear you sometimes.'

'I didn't know I did that,' Miquel said.

'Do you have bad dreams?' Manolo asked him.

'Not really. I often dream that my brother is here and we are much younger.'

'You don't shout, but you cry, never for long,' Manolo said.

'I will try to keep quiet.'

'Don't worry.'

They began to talk about Miquel's mother's disappearance and how she might be found. Manolo kept his voice low and seemed to consider everything very carefully. Miquel told him that Jordi did not know anything about her disappearance. They had received a letter from him, saying he was in Valladolid, to which his father had replied saying there was no news. When Manolo did not respond to this, Miquel knew that he was not asleep but weighing up what he had just been told.

'Your father is wrong,' he said eventually.

'I know,' Miquel said, 'but I can't write to Jordi myself telling him. It's not my job. How could I tell him in a letter what has happened?'

Manolo said nothing; by the quality of his silence Miquel could see that he had made a clear judgement. They lay there saying nothing until Miquel knew that Manolo had fallen asleep.

He himself slept for a while, and then was woken by the wind. It felt, in its fierce whistling menace, that it was preparing to lift the house from its foundations or blow the roof off, or cut through the windows and swirl frantically into each room, dragging sleepers from their beds in its wake. He listened to its howling and the flat rhythm of Manolo's breathing and knew that he would not sleep. Soon, one of the barn doors began to bang; he knew from the sound which one it was, and he knew that he should have put stones against it earlier to secure it in place. He found his clothes in the dark and went downstairs to dress so that he would not disturb Manolo. His boots were in the hall.

It was snowing again, the flakes were being whipped in every direction by the wind. He held his hand over his eyes to stop the wind blinding him. His torch was useless. He made his way down slowly, moving over the packed ice on which a covering of fresh snow had formed. The door was still banging. He found the stones he had used before and put them in place, holding the door firmly shut, and then he made his way back to the house.

6

The sun shone during the days that followed, but the wind still blew. Miquel resumed his old route, to Santa Magdalena without any difficulty, and then trying to walk along the military road where snow was banked up in all its new contours. On one of those days as he went back towards the village, with about half an hour left to go, he saw Manolo coming towards him, he had brought him some bread and ham and some biscuits. Miquel was surprised at how changed he was for the rest of the journey, how light he was, and happy that Manolo had thought of meeting him. The next day, as he was setting off, he asked Manolo if he would come again to meet him and Manolo said he would. He was already planning to do so, he said.

Miquel found that this picture of Manolo standing by the stove saying these words stayed with him more as he walked than any thoughts about his father or Jordi, or where his mother's body might be discovered.

His father was making money from his work with Bernat and all the talk now was of expanding the stone-cutting business. He began to pay Manolo a small sum of money every week and this seemed to make him more cheerful during the time he spent in the kitchen while making no obvious difference to Manolo. On a Saturday night, when Manolo had been a month in the house, Miquel's father announced that it was bath night. His family, he told Manolo, differed from every other family in the village, as indeed from the beasts in the fields, because they regularly took a bath, usually once every two weeks, but because of what had occurred in the house, they had neglected performing their proper ablutions, a matter he now wished to rectify.

His father showed Manolo where the bright tin bath with the long back was kept, and together they carried it into the kitchen. He explained that Manolo's job was to fill the large pot and two of the saucepans with water and bring them to the boil, and mix this water with cold water. That would be enough for his bath. Then Manolo was to put more water on to boil, he said, and when the first bath had been taken, some of the water could be removed and replaced by more clean hot water for Miquel and later for Manolo. Then finally, his father explained, amusing himself, it seemed, greatly as he spoke, the water could be thrown out for the dog to drink. And each of them would also need clean clothes and underclothes, he added, to change into once the bathing was over.

Miquel was surprised that his father saw fit to include Manolo in the bath. Before, he and Jordi had boiled the water and changed the water, while their mother had remained out of the room. Finally, they had boiled water for her and filled a new bath for her, leaving her special soap and sponge on the chair, and a special towel, before they and their father had gone upstairs to offer her full privacy.

Manolo put three towels on a frame in front of the roaring fire; he closed the shutters, and, as the water in the saucepans began to boil, he poured the water into the bath and then refilled the saucepans. As the big pot boiled and his father began to undress, Miquel left the room. This was what he had always done, allowing his father as much privacy as he could. It was strange, he thought, leaving Manolo in there with his naked father, ministering to him, but Manolo, he knew, had a way of managing everything, of making sure that nothing he did was ever the cause of complaint.

When he came back to the kitchen, his father told him that he was almost finished and presently stood up in the bath waiting for Manolo to bring him the towel. Miquel had never watched his father like this before, his long legs, much stronger-looking than he had imagined, his fleshy penis and the pouch underneath larger and more real. His father stood in the firelight drying himself as though he were on display, as Manolo fussed around him, putting a mat under his feet, putting some dry thin wood on the fire and beginning to prepare Miquel's bath.

When his father left the room, Miquel stripped to his shorts, tested the temperature of the water, and then he slipped off his shorts and sat into the hot bath, half clean water and half the water used by his father. Before Jordi left they had a joke together, that their father had pissed in the water, and that Miquel was going to piss too, or had just done so, and Jordi would be thus left to soak in copious quantities of the family's urine. Jordi used to cringe, demanding a full bath of clean hot water, being told by Miquel that, since he was the youngest, that would be impossible.

Miquel did not think that Manolo would find this funny. He washed himself as Manolo began to boil more water for his own bath. He had observed Manolo looking at him as he lowered himself into the water. Manolo hovered close to the bath as Miquel washed himself. They could hear Miquel's father moving around in the room above. Miquel knew that he would not come back into the room until the bathing was finished.

As he stood up in the water, Manolo came towards him with the warm towel. Miquel stood shivering facing the fire as Manolo dried his back and his neck and torso, rubbing hard and then handing him the towel so Miquel could finish drying himself.

Manolo's own water was hot now; he cleared out some of the old water and then poured more from the saucepans and the big pot into the bath. As Miquel sat and dressed himself, he watched Manolo strip with his back to him, not facing him until he was naked. His shoulders were much broader than Miquel had ever noticed in the bedroom, the muscles on his shoulders and back more developed, his torso and buttocks completely hairless, but his thick, short legs covered in dark hair. He moved slowly, almost gracefully, towards the bath, seeming to be utterly alert to Miquel's eyes watching him.

7

Since his father was now travelling every day with Josep Bernat, Miquel told Manolo that he could come earlier to meet him if he wanted, if he had time, and thus Miquel would not have to walk back all the distance on his own. He also told him to take food for himself and a bottle of water so they could both find a place in the sun and eat together. At night now, he looked forward to going to the bedroom and being alone with Manolo, talking to him for a while before they went asleep.

On one of these days as they were walking back, examining how the snow lay in ridges and banks, they heard shots being fired from the trees up above Santa Magdalena. The shots, which came in quick succession, echoed against the far hills so that it was impossible to be sure precisely where they had come from. Miquel remembered that a jeepload of men, including Foix and Castellet, had passed him earlier on the road and he had seen their empty jeep with a trailer parked at the hermitage at Santa Magdalena itself.

The shots seemed to disturb everything, the bird life scattered; every living thing, he knew, would have sought shelter in fright and panic. He and Manolo stopped to listen as more shots, four or five this time, rang out. Suddenly, he began to choke back tears. These men could easily be hunting in the space where his mother had died. She could easily have walked off the road just here, mistaking a blanket of whiteness for the way forward. Miquel did not want them to find her, their dogs smelling and licking her. As more shots sounded, he moved fast, Manolo coming unwillingly behind him. When Manolo asked him why he was going back towards them, Miquel did not answer. For one second he had had a vision of her alive here, running in terror from them, desperate to avoid being shot. As they made their way up the slopes behind the church, they heard shouts and the barking of the dogs and three further shots from the same rifle, a brief and decisive interval between each one. When they heard a shriek and then a cry, Miquel signalled to Manolo to move faster until a sudden shout stopped them.

'Hey, you!' It was Foix's voice. 'Get away from here! Do you want to get shot?'

'What are you doing here?' Miquel shouted back. 'Why don't you go and shoot some place else?'

'We're killing wild boars, it's men's work. You and your little kitchen boy'll be very sorry if you don't go back to the road.'

Manolo pulled at Miquel's jacket, signalling to him to come with him now. They moved slowly down through the snow, walking with a difficulty Miquel had not known when they were climbing, finding ice under the snow, but getting away as fast as they could from the hunters.

They walked back without speaking, Manolo's hand on Miquel's shoulder. There were no more shots. After a time, they heard the jeep approaching and stood out of the way. As it nosed forward, the men inside had a strange, guilty, excited look. They slowed as they passed and Miquel could see the raw thrill in their faces. On the trailer, lying huddled against each other, were four wild boars seeping blood, heavy with death, thrown there, fat, substantial, burrowing creatures, the most powerful animals in the cold dark world just a short time before, but utterly beyond it now, gristle and meat and bone and dead staring eyes, the trailer carrying them leaking blood into the snow in single drops, and then, when the trailer shifted sideways, in a small dense red puddle.

Miquel began to sob as he walked along, allowing Manolo to hold him and comfort him. For the first time in a while he felt the sharp certainty of his mother's disappearance; the idea that when she was found she would not be alive appeared to him as brutal fact. She would not be returning to them. Finding her, he thought, would mean nothing; looking for her was pointless. He stopped crying after a while and kept close to Manolo, who brushed casually against him as they walked through the slush and muck of the road.

'You are lucky, you know,' Manolo said to him.

Miquel did not reply.

'You are lucky that this has already happened to you, your mother's going, that it cannot come again.'

'I wish she was at home, alive,' Miquel said.

'Yes, but you would always dread that this blow was going to come, her death, now you are free of it. It has happened. It cannot happen again.'

'Don't talk like that,' Miquel said.

'In the last house where I stayed,' Manolo said, 'the old man died and all his children came, some of them were old themselves. And even though he was old and dying for a long time, all of them cried for days. Weeks later I would find the woman of the house crying. And when her sister came they cried, and when her brother came they cried even more. I knew that no one would ever make me cry. There is no one who could die whose death would make me cry. No one. And I am grateful for that, and that will never change. My parents died before I could remember, my father even before I was born. I have no memory of them. I have no brothers and sisters, and I have no feeling for my uncles and cousins. Every time I watch someone with a person they are connected with, I always feel sorry for them. It is better not to have it. You are lucky now that she cannot be taken from you again.'

Miquel looked around him and knew that he could embrace Manolo for as long as he pleased on this empty road and could hold him as closely as he wished. He put his arms around him and felt the warmth of him as he moved his hands under his jacket. He could feel the sweat on Manolo's shirt and he could feel his heart thumping. He pulled at the shirt and then placed his hands on the warm skin of Manolo's back. Manolo hunched towards him, letting their bodies lock, he buried his head in Miquel's shoulder but he kept his hands by his sides as though they were stones.

8

When Manolo pulled back the shutters the following morning, Miquel saw that the sky was blue and the morning sun was strong enough to have caused the icicles which had hung from the eaves to begin dripping and breaking. In the kitchen, Josep Bernat was sitting with his father, insisting that the weather had turned, that the haze over the far mountains meant the real thaw had begun. That day as he walked, the abiding sound was of ice breaking and unloosening, snow melting and slipping away, and water flowing in channels at the edge of the road. Through the binoculars he could see the whiteness of snow becoming mere patches in the distance.

The following day his uncle came from Pallosa to say

that the snow on the slopes between the village and Coll del So had begun to melt. In the villages, he said, they were all watching for the vultures who would surely move upwards to Coll del So as the days got better. The villagers would follow the vultures once they appeared, he said, and Miquel and his father and their neighbours should do the same. It would not be long now, he said, before the snow and the ice covering her body would go. He would like to find her before the wild boars and the wild dogs and the vultures, he said, but it was the vultures who would come first. It was the vultures they had to watch for.

Most of the military road was passable after a few days of higher temperatures. Miquel shifted between the fierce longing which came over him once darkness fell to have her back to them in any guise and the knowledge that the time she was lost to them was nearly ended, the snow was going to yield his mother up. He thought of her face; he hoped he might see it again the way it was, as though she were sleeping or sitting by the kitchen window. As he walked, he thought how much he would like to see her smile.

He could walk for hours now without having his progress impeded by packed snow and ice, and when tired pushed himself to go further, knowing that once he was beyond Santa Magdalena there was nowhere he could rest. When he had walked long distances, he found that his imagination was vivid with images and scenes as though the air itself were a drug that led mild fantasies to seem entirely real. Sometimes, in the unsettling magic of this, he allowed himself to entertain moments where he was not himself, he was not Miquel, he was somebody else and yet she was coming towards him, dazed and wondering what had happened to her in all that time she was sleeping. She would recognize him immediately, crying out, not as her son searching for her, but as her own father when she was a little girl, her father come looking for her. She would run towards him waiting to be lifted, and he would kiss her and lift her up, the girl who had been lost, her small gloves keeping her hands warm, her old green coat with the fur collar, her snow hat. Only her face was freezing, her eyes were wet with cold, she was trying to smile even though her teeth were chattering.

He would take her down to the old house in Pallosa, to the search party cheering that she had been found, to her brother waiting for her, to the warm fire and the old comfortable bed. Once, he began to imagine Manolo there too, wearing an apron, preparing a hot drink, all pale and anxious. But somehow that image failed him. Manolo did not belong to the scene.

The first vultures appeared in the late morning in the cold blue sky a week after the thaw had begun. Miquel was already walking, they appeared black and hovering over a patch of earth above Pallosa but below the military road, precisely where he and his father and the rest of them imagined his mother might be. As he watched them carefully through the binoculars, he wondered whether he should walk to the village and find his father, who he knew was close by, and come back this way in the jeep, but he trusted that his father, or someone in the village, would have become alert to the birds of prey and would set out immediately. He also had confidence that his uncle would have already seen them. He believed his uncle's determination that those who had loved her should find her first.

He walked forward, stopping regularly to scrutinize them with the binoculars. Two birds hovered high in the air, not moving. He was not certain how vultures worked, but thought that they needed more than two before they swooped. He did not know how long it would take them to gather once dead prey had been spotted. He hoped that it would take time because he did not want to have to fend them off alone, he did not know how he would be able to struggle against them if more came.

Soon, he noticed another vulture over Coll del So; he knew that it could be seen for miles. The sky was a clear blue without a single speck of cloud; there was no other movement, no other bird life in the sky. As one of them dipped, Miquel moved faster, wondering if he should not cut a stick from one of the trees to strike them with. He calculated that it would take his uncle an hour or more to climb the slopes over which the birds had gathered. His father, if he took the jeep, could move faster. He was afraid now that he would be left to come on the scene alone. The grim, silent, hungry creatures, merciless in the high sky, would hardly be afraid of him. They would do what nature had taught them to do, no matter what Miquel did. He would be no match for them; all he could do was to go rapidly towards the scene over which they flew. Even to be a witness to where they landed would be better than turning now, leaving her to their beaks and claws, leaving her defenceless and helpless.

Two more sailed through the bright air. He stood and fixed them in the binoculars, noting their size and the sheer ugliness of their colour and shape; now there were five of them. He did not know if that would be enough for the ritual of feeding which was built into their dark system, and at what point they would pounce.

Maybe, he thought, their landing might be more ragged in its timing, lazier, less precise. In all the years, he had seen them gather in a group, but he had never seen them feed; they kept away from the villages, and they had no dealings with a healthy flock of sheep. He wished he knew more about them, how to frighten them, or how long they took at their work.

By the time his father's jeep came towards him, two of the vultures had landed and the others, five or six now, were lower in the sky. His father, whose face was frozen in fear and anger and full of vigorous intent, was driving with Josep Bernat in the front passenger seat and Manolo in the back seat. He barely stopped for Miquel. When he got in, he saw that Bernat had two rifles stretched across his lap. His father drove fast and relentlessly towards the birds.

He knew about the eyes, that they pecked your eyes out first, and he supposed they had already done that; perhaps the strongest one, or the fastest, won the right. It could not take long to pull someone's eyes out. There would be no blood, he supposed that her blood would have congealed or drained away. He supposed, too, that they would go for the soft places in her body, leaving her head and her arms and legs for last. He was desperately trying not to cry as the jeep stopped with a jerk and they got out and began to scamper as best they could down the slope.

Some distance below there was a flat clearing, and this was where the birds had gathered. Miquel could not believe that his mother had ended here, she could not have fallen in as open a place, he thought, and, in any case, the passes which led down to Pallosa were further along. He handed his father the glasses and, when Bernat had also looked through them, he took them himself and began to study the scene. The birds had not fully settled around their prey. They were large flapping creatures, filthy-looking, hitting against each other as though they were blind. Then they fastened on a spot and began to peck, pushing one another out of the way. As his father and Bernat edged slowly forward and Manolo stayed near him, he was transfixed by the scene the binoculars magnified. The vultures were feasting on piles of viscera, snatching pieces away, eating with greed and relish and then barging back in for more. He focused on one of them putting one claw down hard for leverage so it could all the better tear the flesh from her with its beak. He dropped the binoculars, crying out, and ran towards his father and Bernat with Manolo following him.

As they grew close, the birds began to move away, but in their resentful flapping, they had left a smell in their wake. The smell was sour and horrible, he thought, but it was not the smell of rotting flesh but the stench of something living. It was the smell of foul energy, the birds themselves, their pungent odour which came, he thought, from their digesting what was rotten and dead.

Miquel almost smiled when he saw what they had gathered around. He had been ready to witness his mother's entrails poured out as though she were an old and abandoned animal, and he had been ready to protect her as best he could. The vultures had come all this way, he saw, not to find his mother but to peck a large dog, like a hunting dog, down to its bones. They must have had a hungry winter, he thought, as he stood back.

As one of the vultures flew insolently over them, Miquel saw his father lift the gun. From this close range, his father fired one shot from the rifle at the bird, the one with the scaliest wings and the most rabid energy; he sent it tumbling downwards with the force of the bullet, while the other vultures flew upwards or flapped their clumsy wings and moved angrily back.

The injured bird, lying almost upside down, began to screech, tried to rise and fell back. Suddenly, it managed to lift its head, which was raw and unbowed, utterly alive, the eyes indignant and sharp, the nostrils almost breathing fire within the vicious beak. The vulture saw them, and all its sullen hatred for them, its savage gaze, its fierce panic, caught Miquel, as though it were directed at him and him only, as though his secret spirit had been waiting all its life for such recognition. The dying bird was beyond human in its grief and its injury, screeching still in pain. Miquel did not know why he began to edge towards it, but he quickly found that Manolo was holding him from behind, preventing him moving further as his father lifted the gun again. Miquel leaned backwards towards Manolo, seeking the warmth of him, looking for some grim comfort as the next shot rang out. Manolo held him hard to make sure that he did not move any closer to the dying bird and the carcass, half torn asunder now, no use to anyone.

Afterword

I wrote the story 'A Long Winter' twenty years ago. In February and March 2005 I stayed in a small house in the landscape where the story is set. I witnessed the *burufa*, the surface snow that is swirled about by the wind to create the impression that there is a blizzard. Some days, as I walked along narrow roads and snow-covered paths, I heard the hunters. One day, a jeep came by with a trailer in which lay a few dead wild boars.

The wooden door into the yard often banged at night. One night, as I went out into the freezing dark to close it, I consoled myself by planning to put that small moment into the story once I started work again in the morning.

More than a decade earlier, with a friend, I had bought

a run-down barn in a small village in the Pallars, in the Catalan province of Lleida, a village more than four thousand feet above sea level. We had set about making the barn habitable. We had a small yard, but no garden. Beside the house there was a long wild garden space that didn't seem to be attached to a house. Eventually we located the man who owned it. He was in his seventies and lived over the mountain.

Going to see him became an annual ritual, as each year he refused to consider selling this small plot. But he was hospitable and polite, and the journey itself, on an old dirt road high in the Pyrenees, was beautiful enough in itself to make the journey worthwhile. Even the names of the villages had their own resonance: Ars; Civís; Os de Civís.

In the summer of 2004, without notice, the man who owned the garden made a visit with his son. The old man made clear that he wanted to sell everything he owned around the village. This would include two fields and a small part of the forest and a few other tiny plots of land. It would also include the garden.

Although we looked at the other land he wished to sell, it was only the garden that interested us. But the man was having none of it. He wanted us to buy the whole lot. And he had a price in mind. Nothing we could do convinced him to separate the garden from the rest, or to lower the price. His point was that we had come to him year in, year out seeking to buy land from him. Now here it was, what was our problem? Were we not serious?

It would be easy to cut a door from the house into this garden that was like a long terrace. Towards the middle sat a small ruin of some sort, with no roof and a lot of earth and scrub inside the broken-down stone walls. There was nothing much that could be done with this.

That evening, when the deal had been done, we had a visit from a man who lived in a house lower down in the village. He went through the various fields and plots of land included in the sale. And, almost casually, he mentioned that the ruin in the garden was once a house, and the mother of the man who had sold us the land had been born and brought up in that house.

'That was a terrible business,' he said, but would not

expand. Clearly, something had happened in that house now ruined in that garden.

Over the next while, I pieced together the outline of the story. The mother of the old man who sold us the land had been born in that house. On marrying, she went to live in another village over the mountain. It is unclear if she really was a heavy drinker, but that became the rumour after her death, a death that occurred when she left the house in her husband's village abruptly one winter's day to walk to the village where she had been born.

The high Pyrenees are at their most dangerous on early winter days when the sky is blue and the sun is shining. It is on such days that the first snowstorm comes, and it can come very fast. And when the snow falls like this, it is there for the winter. The thaw might not come until April.

Thus, since she walked out of her house on a day like that, and since she did so alone, then the woman would be buried by the snow. And most likely her body would not be discovered until the spring.

The story stayed in my mind. It struck me that, as an outsider, I might never have discovered what the ruin in the garden was or had been. And if we were to restore it or make it habitable it would surely carry remnants, clues, echoes, traces.

But then I realized that really it wouldn't. Ideas about the dead inhabiting domestic spaces belong to ghost stories, imagined experiences, legends and films. I could, if I wanted, write scenes in a story where someone – perhaps even this woman who died in the snow – made sounds – tapping sounds, low howling sounds – at night, thus unsettling an Irishman who had had the temerity to restore an old house. But such scenes would be manufactured, made up.

The story nonetheless remained in my mind. For a while I had been thinking about the connection between the shape of a story in fiction and the shape of a ballad. Some lines and details in a ballad – 'It was early in the spring' – offer a sense of the inevitable, the seasonal, the expected. And then the ballad can go anywhere. It should be possible to summarize, I thought, or indeed dramatize the material in any novel using the ballad stanza form. If it wouldn't work as a ballad, then it probably wouldn't work as a story.

For example, the opening stanza in 'Middlemarch: a ballad' might read:

> *He was twice her age and buried in books*
> *And suffered hard from nerves and gout*
> *But she took a shine to him-o*
> *And they were married before that year was out.*

The story I began to imagine had winter and spring, it was set in a remote place, it had a body that could not be found, and a search for the body, first as an emergency and then as ritual. It had a mother and her son. It had a forest, it had snow.

> *He went out in the hardened snow*
> *In those dark, forbidding days.*
> *She was deep in nature then*
> *Hidden from his grieving gaze.*

At first, I imagined all the family going in search of the mother. Then I decided to remove one brother from the picture in order to make the story starker and more intense. For a while, the perspective was the mother's, the story was her walk in the snow. Sometimes, ideas like that would last a while and then they would fade, dissolve. And another way of seeing the drama or setting up the point of view would emerge.

At that time, I had written some stories that would eventually appear in the volume *Mothers and Sons*. I had also written the first chapter of the novel that became *Nora Webster*. It occurred to me then, almost as a way of making that title *Mothers and Sons* more solid, that I could give all the point of view to the son.

This meant that everything would be seen by him, registered by him, known by him, noticed by him, remembered by him, felt by him. However, he would not tell the story; it would not use his voice. Instead, it would use the lens and the prism of his perspective. The style would be slow, immersive, third-person intimate. The theory of this is that the reader enters into the spirit of the protagonist after a few pages and begins thereafter to see the world as though they are him, or as though they are close to him.

I worked in longhand every day, with much erasure and revision at the beginning. And then sometimes I could write a few pages that would need hardly any changes. The very weather in the story was happening outside my window. The cold and the ice and the packed snow and the dulled sky looked as though they would never change. Some of the roads had been cleared by snowploughs and some of the paths made easier by use. But walking on any slope was dangerous as there could be packed ice underneath. And the higher you went, the deeper the snow.

At first, it seemed easier and more dramatic to allow the disputes between Miquel's father and his neighbours to have their roots in the Spanish Civil War, but this eventually made no sense. And it made the story political in a way that I didn't want. Instead, the problems between people in the village came from smaller, more local disputes about fences and water rights.

As I packed to come to Catalonia to write the story, I had removed some CDs from their cases and put them into a CD holder for travelling. This meant that I had a CD of Bryn Terfel singing Schubert songs without the CD case and without the notes on the songs or the lyrics. I never played music when I was working, but during breaks or when coming back from walks or at night I began to play one Schubert song over and over without knowing even its name.

A few months earlier I had interviewed Terfel for a magazine. He told me about coming to London from rural Wales to study when he was eighteen, taking no part in the social life of the city, simply practising, working on his voice. In London, he worked with a single teacher on English art songs. He was meant to do nothing else. But he knew for some time that he would have to tell his teacher, a most sensitive and dedicated man, that he must expand his repertoire.

I wrote: 'It was a tough decision to make after three years, and he still looks sad when he talks about it, to change teachers, to expand his horizons at the school. He dreaded those days, he says, leading up to the time when he had to tell Arthur that he was moving on.'

That move led eventually to his work with those Schubert songs. The one I had been listening to is called

'Litanei auf das Fest Allerseelen' ('Litany for the Feast of All Souls'). Its first stanza reads:

> *May all souls rest in peace;*
> *those whose fearful torment is past;*
> *those whose sweet dreams are over;*
> *those sated with life, those barely born,*
> *who have left this world:*
> *may all souls rest in peace!*

I had presumed it to be a slow, sad love song. Or a song about a stranger alone in a new place. I did not know it was a prayer for the dead.

I was aware of the form 'A Long Winter' would take. It would not be a novel. And it would not be a short story as I understood the term. It would live in a place in between. I smiled at the thought of a novella because I had come to the conclusion that a novella is something that no one wants.

Maybe no one would want what I was writing either. It was bleak, it was set in a remote place. If there was a gay man in the story, his sexuality seemed to lead to dull disappointment rather than excitement. Later that year, when the movie *Brokeback Mountain*, based on Annie Proulx's story, came out, I consoled myself that, like hers, my story was all mountain but, unlike hers, there was hardly any brokeback.

For some reason, the idea that 'A Long Winter' would remain hidden or live in the shadows satisfied me or impelled me to make it better or darker or more intense and exact. It was published first as a limited edition. And then in late 2006 it was published at the end of the book of stories *Mothers and Sons*.

Colm Tóibín, January 2025